Praise for

THE LAST STAR WARDEN:
Tales of ADVENTURE and MYSTERY
from Frontier Space
Volume I

"*The Last Star Warden* is exactly what it looks like: a rollicking collection of space western stories. McCuiston delivers big with plenty of imagination and thrills. He pays homage to a western classic formula while injecting enough delightful alien weirdness to justify the intergalactic setting. The Warden and Quantum are unashamedly heroic heroes doing what's right in an unforgiving universe. Highly recommended."

~ Bryce Beattie,

Editor of *StoryHack Action & Adventure* and author of *Swordcrossed Frostbite*

"The Last Star Warden—a.k.a. 'The Phantom Lawman' or 'The Ghost of the Frontier'—finds himself displaced a hundred years into his future and facing off against numerous foes and dangers he never dreamed possible: a derelict space station haunted by vengeful ghosts, a behemoth corporate-built machine that feasts on entire stars, and a merciless prison ship among them. Armed only with his twin Comet pistols and his former-enemy-turned-sidekick Quantum for backup, the Last Star Warden meets all with steely grace and nobility—and a rare and refreshing level of pure, pulpy fun. Jason McCuiston's excellent book of adventures reads like a time warp back to boyhood Saturdays when classic Science Fiction played all afternoon on UHF. A fantastic experience!"

~ Gregory L. Norris,

Author of the *Gerry Anderson's Into Infinity* novels by Anderson Entertainment

The Last Star Warden:
Tales of ADVENTURE and MYSTERY From Frontier Space

Written and Illustrated by
Jason J. McCuiston

From
Dark Owl Publishing, LLC

Arizona

Cover design by Melrose Dowdy
melrosedowdy.com

Visit us on our website at:
www.darkowlpublishing.com

Also From Dark Owl Publishing

Anthologies
A Celebration of Storytelling
The anthological festival of tales.

Something Wicked This Way Rides
Where genre fiction meets the Wild West.
(coming July 1, 2021)

Collections
The Dark Walk Forward
A harrowing collection of frightful stories from John S. McFarland.

No Lesser Angels, No Greater Devils
Beautiful and haunting stories collected from Laura J. Campbell.
(coming May 1, 2021)

Novels
The Keeper of Tales
An epic fantasy adventure by Jonathon Mast.

Just About Anyone
High fantasy comedy from the twisted mind of Carl R. Jennings.
(Coming September 1, 2021)

Buy the books for Kindle and in paperback
www.darkowlpublishing/the-bookstore

For
Alex, Connor, and Aidan.

Table of Contents

The Sun Smasher

Adrift somewhere in the depths of Frontier Space, the *Ranger VII* was in a bad way, and the Last Star Warden knew it.

Riddled with blast holes and down to one of its three atomic engines, the sleek, silver patrol ship needed an overhaul, and fast. The two-man craft had been the pinnacle of human technological endeavors over a century ago, but now looked as if it had escaped from a museum. But for all that, the ship had just bested a flotilla of six modern pirate vessels, freeing up a sector of the vast Frontier for safe space travel.

The *Ranger VII* had accomplished this feat due in large part to the daring skill of its pilot.

At the moment, that pilot wasn't much better off. Still wearing his blue and silver body-tight spacesuit, the bruised and battered man at the antiquated ship's controls set course for an "Undoc" system. Like his ship, the Warden was a relic of another time, but due to the vagaries of quantum physics, multi-dimensional realities, and dark-matter wormholes, he now found himself roaming the wilds of the modern Frontier, carrying on a mission all but forgotten over the past hundred years.

"Your injuries are not severe," Quantum said from the copilot seat. "But I would recommend you take some time to recover before engaging in further hostilities."

The Warden spared the blue-skinned alien a square-jawed grin. Quantum was the sole member—at least in this galaxy—of the Mechtechan, an interdimensional race of conquest-oriented masterminds. Quantum's people had tried to invade this reality over a century ago. The ensuing battle—now listed under "The Continuum War" in modern history files—had decimated the Star Wardens, forced the Mechtechan back into their own parallel dimension, and had thrust these two unlikely companions over a century into the future.

Or rather, the present day, the Warden continued to remind himself.

"You needn't worry." The Warden returned his visor-concealed eyes to the control panel. "Judging by the condition of the *Ranger VII*, I won't have the opportunity to pick any more fights for quite some time."

Quantum shook his elongated head, his two antennae wiggling. "If I know you, and I do, you will find a way if there is a fight to be had."

The Warden smiled. Quantum knew him better than anyone else in the galaxy. "Well then, let's find a place to rest and refit so we're ready when that fight comes."

The *Ranger VII* arced across the vast starry firmament, heading for the third brown planet orbiting a white star, a star designated Kleppin according to the newest databases. The absence of artificial satellites or installations on the three moons indicated the planet was neither militarized nor industrialized. Initial scans showed life signs in a populated settlement on a large continent of the northwestern hemisphere.

It was an undocumented world.

"Undocs" were the poor courageous folk who braved the perils of space travel, pirates, alien raiders, and unscrupulous corporate agents to colonize new worlds of the Frontier. This in defiance of the Unified Planetary Council's modern Frontier Preservation Acts. Most of these intrepid colonists did this out of desperation rather than any sense of adventure or opportunity, though there were plenty of outlaws and renegades among them.

The Earth and the Civilized Worlds of the Star Warden's time no longer existed, at least not as he had known them. A lot had changed in the past century.

The ship descended into a rocky clearing about two kilometers south of the large settlement. By the time the *Ranger VII* had finished its landing cycle and come to rest in an upright position, a crowd of locals had gathered outside the radius of the ship's rocket wash. The Warden turned to Quantum with a smile. "Time to meet the neighbors."

"Perhaps you should go alone. My presence might alarm them and make things unnecessarily... unpleasant."

The Warden shook his head. "One thing I know about these folks: They don't like any stranger more or less than any other. They know they're not supposed to be here, and all they care about is whether or not we're here to remind them of that. Since I don't cotton to these new anti-settlement laws, I don't intend to do so."

Quantum sighed and followed the injured Warden to the ship's lowered gangplank. He hung back at the top, however. As expected, the colonists were all armed with varmint guns, rock cutters, and antique service carbines. There were a couple hand blasters in the mix as well.

"Who are you and what do you want?" A dark-skinned woman in the front rank wore a heavy salvager's spacesuit and held a blaster at her side. The armed crowd grumbled nervously behind her.

The Warden raised his gloved hands in supplication, careful to keep them well away from the twin Comet blaster pistols holstered on his own belt. He smiled at the crowd, though his eyes were masked by the dark visor attached to his suit's skullcap. "My name doesn't matter anymore." His deep voice carried in the thin atmosphere. "I was once a lawman entrusted with keeping the Frontier safe. I was lost in time for a while, but now I'm back to continue that job."

He turned to indicate the ship. "In fact, I've just come from a tussle with some pirates. As you can see, my ship didn't make it through unscathed, so we'd just like to borrow some real estate, and maybe some parts if you can spare them, to affect repairs. That is, if it's all the same to you."

"*We?*" The woman asked.

The Warden turned and nodded. "My friend. His name is Quantum; at least, that's what I call him."

Quantum descended the plank, standing at least a head and a half taller than most Earthmen. The Mechtechan's pale blue skin was less shocking than his elongated skull, nose-less face, pointed ears, and the two antennae swiveling at his crown. If not for the large, almost childlike eyes and small, upturned mouth, he might have appeared quite monstrous.

No one raised a weapon or gasped with fear. A lone voice came from the rear: "What kind is that? Never seen one o' them before."

Quantum sniffed, the thin nostrils between his antennae closing quickly. "I should imagine not. I am the last of my kind left in this—"

"He's a stranger, just like me," the Warden said. "Neither of us wants any trouble. We just want permission to fix our ship, and then we'll be on our way."

"I thought you'd be taller." The woman holstered her blaster. "I've heard of you. The Last Star Warden. They say you're a ghost what haunts the Frontier, punishing them what does evil in the badlands of space. You don't look like no ghost to me. Just a man too dumb to run from a fight." She said this last with a smile, which softened her face considerably.

The Warden returned the expression. "No argument there."

"Well, I reckon it can't do no harm to have an extra do-gooder around for a spell." She turned to the crowd. "What say ye: Can they stay 'til their ship's fixed?"

There was a low murmur, before a slow chorus of *ayes* rippled through the crowd. Soon after, the throng dispersed as the hard-working folk got back to the jobs that ensured their families' continued survival.

The woman stepped forward. "My name's Ara Halum. I guess I'm what you'd call the mouthpiece of this here settlement, mostly 'cause I don't know when to keep mine shut. But if you'd like more than space rations for dinner, you two are welcome at our place. The big farm on the west side of the compound. Be there about eighteen hundred hours or so." She held up a wrist chrono so the Warden could sync his to local time.

"We'd be obliged, ma'am."

Karen Reeves, SuperCorp Senior Vice President in charge of Research and Development, stood on the bridge of the *Star Sequencer 1*, the prototype solar energy harvester that had been her pet project for the past decade. Her heart raced as the gigantic ship thrummed with immeasurable power. With a nod, she gave the command to activate the siphoning engines. Her dark eyes flicking to the forward view screen, she watched as the big yellow sun flared and pulsed, its near-infinite power being consumed by the ship. *Her* ship. Her masterpiece, the pinnacle of her corporate career.

Engineering reported in. "Siphoning engines holding at seventy-five percent intake. Containment cells successfully filling. All systems satisfactory."

In a matter of minutes, the star faded in color. The inner planets froze and died as the sun weakened, its life pulled into the mechanical guts of the *Star Sequencer 1*, stored to later be sold in the Civilized Worlds at a considerable profit. There were countless stars in the Frontier, countless opportunities for more and more profits.

"Ms. Reeves," the helmsman said. "We're picking up a ship. It appears to be a short-range Undoc vessel from the fourth planet. It is transmitting a distress signal and making for the system's Einstein-Rosen bridge."

"Jam its coms and send a detachment to capture it." Karen smiled, still aglow in the first successful test of her passion project. "We can't have anyone or anything hindering our maiden voyage. This is still a top secret operation, after all."

The Warden and Quantum spent the next few hours assessing the damage and running diagnostics. Most of the damage was superficial, but one of the *Ranger VII*'s engines had a crack in the fusion chamber that needed sealing. Fortunately, Quantum was immune to radiation and could affect the repairs, but it would take time.

"Well, that's the dinner bell." The Warden donned a clean spacesuit. "Most of the hull plates have been patched or replaced and the batteries are recharging. Time to accept Miss Halum's hospitality."

Quantum's face pinched into his version of a frown. "I do not like the idea of leaving the ship alone and unguarded. Those people could come back looking for salvage, and with that reactor damaged, they could be exposed to high doses of radiation."

The Warden shrugged, lowering his visor over his eyes. "Suit yourself. I'll bring you something back."

As the Warden descended the gangplank, Quantum called after him. "Preferably a few high-grade ingots of fusion-resistant PermaSteel."

"I'll see what I can do."

The Warden looked up at the starry night sky as he hiked the rugged distance to the settlement. His thoughts wandered back to the now-forgotten war that had occurred only a few months ago for him and Quantum, the war that had sent them spiraling through space and time. The war that had cut them off—possibly forever—from their own respective homes and people. Although they had met as enemies, he and the blue alien were now the best of friends.

"Strange how the saving of a life when you're meant to do the opposite can make all the difference in the world," the Warden said to himself.

The Undoc settlement sprawled in an orderly array of structures cobbled together from the original colony ship and local materials. Barns, cattle pens, corrals, and chicken coops huddled beside craft shops, huts, houses, and other domiciles. A primitive existence by the standards of the modern space age, but the Warden could not deny the charm of the communal life, where neighbors were as close as family.

Of course, he was a stranger and was regarded as such. The farmers and craftsmen paused in their labors as he entered the ring of buildings and made his way to the Halum residence. Women pulled their small children closer, while the older kids got as close as they dared to steal a glance at the "Last Star Warden." Though no one returned the gesture, he smiled and nodded politely.

A rusty cybernetic shepherd trotted up and sniffed his hand. The Warden knelt and petted the mechanical canine until its tail wagged with a creaking noise.

"You the Warden, mister?"

He looked up to see a short, thin, green-skinned boy with solid yellow eyes and brown hair frowning at him. The boy's younger sister stood behind him, a smile on her green face. A face that reminded him of someone he had just met.

"I am," the Warden said as he stood. "And I'm guessing you'd be the Halum children. Your mother invited me to dinner."

The boy stuck out his right hand. "I'm Jes, and this is my sister, Wan. That's Tycho," he indicated the robotic dog. "Ma sent us to fetch you."

The Warden shook the lad's hand. "Well met, Jes Halum." He touched his visor as a greeting to the girl. "Well met, Wan Halum. I thank you for your hospitality."

The girl's yellow eyes widened. "Where's the blue man?"

The Warden laughed. "Quantum? He's decided to take a nap at the ship. Perhaps if your parents say it is all right, you can come out and I'll introduce you tomorrow."

This softened Jes Halum's demeanor. With a smile, he said, "Come along, Mister Warden. Ma's making fried chicken, cornbread, and greens. Don't want 'em getting cold."

The Warden's stomach growled at the thought of eating something that hadn't spent at least a decade in a freeze-dried foil packet. He hadn't had fried chicken since he left Earth for his last mission, some months ago by his internal clock. Even the possibilities of cold leftovers sounded like a feast at the moment. "Please lead the way, young Master Halum."

He was not disappointed in the culinary skills of Mrs. Halum, nor in her family's gracious hospitality.

"I was a smuggler," Bin Halum said as the adults sat around the table after dinner, the children doing homework in their rooms. The green-skinned Senesian was short and stocky, and aside from his hairless green body and yellow eyes, he resembled a muscular human. "In the days following the last war between the Sol corporations and my people, there was lots of money to be had moving wartime goods—weapons, munitions, medical supplies, logistical equipment, even reinforced uniforms—from one side of the galaxy to the other. There was also good money to be made in trafficking refugees."

The Senesian's face softened as he held out a hand to his human wife. Ara Halum smiled and squeezed her husband's hand when he said, "That's how we met. I was the 'ruthless space pirate' and she was the loud-mouthed head of this ragtag group of displaced colonists. They'd contracted my crew to get them off one of the worlds annexed by SuperCorp following the peace accords. When I went soft on her, my first mate mutinied, and we had a fight on our hands…"

Ara cleared her throat. "We lost some good people, but were able to find this rock and stake our claim. That was almost ten years ago, and we're finally seeing progress. Our crops and livestock are flourishing as the terraforming takes hold. Our existence here is now becoming viable. By the time Jes and Wan are grown, it might even be prosperous."

The Warden nodded at the story and its apparent happy ending. Placing his coffee cup on the table, he said, "Well, I'm glad things are working out for you. I know it can't be easy out here on your own, with no one to call if things get bad. It's a risky situation, for sure, but the more I learn about how things work in this day and age, the more I understand why folks like you take those risks."

A blinding flare of light flashed through the window.

"What's that?" The Warden jumped to his feet, thinking of the damaged reactor on the *Ranger VII* and Quantum.

"A meteorite?" Ara suggested, spotting the smoke trail in the atmosphere.

"No. A ship," Bin corrected, reaching for his coat. A moment later they heard the thumping boom of an explosion. "A crash landing."

The Warden and the Halums led a crowd of colonists toward the crash site to the west of the settlement. Crossing a low ridge covered with scrub, they saw the debris field and the small crater where most of the fuselage lay in a crumpled heap of burning metal. The Warden was grateful the pilot had jettisoned the atomic engines before entering the atmosphere. A nuclear incident this close to the settlement would have been fatal to all concerned.

"You recognize the ship type?" Bin asked.

"No. Doesn't look military though. Or even corporate."

"Over here!" someone shouted. "Got a survivor over here!"

The Warden and the Halums ran to the semicircle of colonists. In the center of the ring sat a man strapped to an ejection seat. His spacesuit was torn and bloody, his clear GlasSteel helmet cracked. But his pale grey eyes blinked with alertness. He tried to remove his helmet, but both arms were broken.

"Here!" Ara carried her first-aid kit to the pilot's side. "Stay with us. You'll be fine."

The Warden eased the man's helmet off. "Take it easy. Long, deep breaths, my friend. You've made it through the worst of it."

"No!" The injured pilot winced as Ara gave him an injection. "The Sun Smasher is coming…!"

As the man faded into unconsciousness, the Warden exchanged confused glances with the Halums. "The Sun Smasher?"

Ara turned to the onlookers. "Help me get him back to the farm. We'll tend to him and maybe he'll be ready to talk come morning."

A sonic boom shook the night sky.

"Looks like another one." Bin Halum watched the glow of a ship entering the upper atmosphere. "And this one's under control. If I had to guess, these might be the folks responsible for this fellow's crash."

The Warden rested his hands on his belted Comets. "Then I'll ask them about this Sun Smasher… Everyone go back to the settlement and get everything locked down tight. I'll see if these newcomers mean trouble. If they do, I'll meet them in kind."

Bin Halum took the Warden's arm as he turned to go. "You can't be serious. By the size of that plume, there could be an entire company of marines on that thing."

The Warden smiled. "You just keep your family and neighbors safe. If I'm not the next person to enter the settlement after lockdown, you know what to do."

The new ship came down on a heading about a kilometer to the north of the crash site, and the Warden headed that way. If Bin was right and there was a full company aboard, they could split up, sending one platoon to the settlement and another to the downed ship. The best way to prevent that was to catch them as soon as they disembarked.

Despite his recent injuries, the Warden was still a fast runner.

He arrived at the edge of the clearing as the transport ship's rocket wash faded and the whining sub-orbital engines cycled down. The Warden walked into the landing zone, hands at his sides and waited for the ship's gangplank to descend. Eight men in faceless, jet-black heavy armor and carrying blaster carbines hurried out to face him. Though the troopers did not raise their weapons, they kept them at the ready.

Noting the SuperCorp logo on the side of the transport and emblazoned on the armored breastplates, the Warden relaxed. A fire team and not a company. Not even real marines, just corporate security. Mercenaries.

"You're not military," the Warden said. "What's a corporation doing this far into the Frontier? Have you got authorization from the Unified Planetary Council?"

The squad leader's trigger finger tapped the frame of his carbine. "Who the hell are you?"

"Just a concerned citizen. You wouldn't happen to know anything about that crash back there, would you?"

The troopers remained silent. But they bristled. They were fighting men, anticipating the promise of violence.

"Okay, what can you tell me about something called a Sun Smasher?"

The mercenary leader raised his helmed chin. "You ask a lot of questions, stranger. I'll tell you right now, the answer to all of them is, it's none of your damn business."

The Warden smiled. "And if I make it my business?"

"Then you are in for one very bad day."

The Warden shook his head. "No need for threats. We can be civilized about this, can't we? I mean, it's not like SuperCorp is running some kind of *illegal* operation out here in the uncharted worlds, is it? *They* aren't violating the Frontier Preservation Acts, are they?"

The troopers glanced at one another and raised their rifles. The leader's finger went for the trigger.

He was dead before he hit the ground.

The Warden drew his Comets and opened fire as soon as the troopers signaled their intent. They were here to mop up, to tie up loose ends for their paymasters. That now included the pilot of the crashed ship and every colonist in the settlement. The Warden had seen enough of corporate mercenaries in this modern age to know that these troopers would not differentiate between men, women, and children. All were just obstacles to the next bonus check.

When the dust settled, the eight SuperCorp grunts lay scattered around the rocky clearing, bleeding into the dirt. The Warden hadn't moved from where he stood. He holstered his pistols and noted the red line across his left side where a blaster bolt had grazed him.

"One more for the collection," he muttered. He checked the bodies before boarding the transport.

"You missed one."

The Warden turned on the gangplank to see Quantum crossing the clearing, his long particle-beam rifle in his hands.

"No, I didn't."

"The one on the far left." The alien tsk'ed at the Warden's new wound. "You know you are not as good a shot with your left hand as you seem to think. It is a good thing I decided to come and have a look when this one came down. Otherwise you would probably be ecosystem-enhancing fertilizer like these fellows."

The Warden shrugged. "Well, maybe I missed him and maybe I didn't. Either way, I'm glad you came just the same. Now, want to help me check this ship's logs? I've got a bad feeling that whoever sent these guys is up to no good, and a heap of it."

"What about that piece of *serratus anterior* you are missing?"

"It'll keep. Something tells me that whatever a Sun Smasher is, it trumps a flesh wound."

It didn't take Quantum long to crack the ship's security system and gain access to not only the ship's logs but also the network to which its computer was attached. It took the Mechtechan genius even less time to access and fully understand the severity of the threat now facing them.

"This is not good." Quantum pulled up the diagnostics on the main screen. "SuperCorp has developed solar siphoning technology on a truly monumental scale. They have an actionable prototype that can completely drain the energy of a star and process it into storable, marketable energy units. They plan to kill stars in the Frontier to sell their energy in the Civilized Systems."

Quantum pulled up another display, showing an expanding rift in space. "It would appear this Sun Smasher—actually the *Star Sequencer 1*—has already been successfully tested in a nearby system, designated Janglu. I suggest that the pilot of the crashed ship was a survivor. I would have to backtrack the drive trail to the connecting Einstein-Rosen bridge to verify this hypothesis, but…"

"No need. My gut tells me you're right."

The Warden stared at the massive ship displayed on the screen. Such a thing would have been impossible to conceive, much less build in his own time. He looked at the dying star system, where six worlds and their moons faced annihilation in the depths of the newborn black hole. How many undocumented settlers had already perished in that system?

"When we first flew to the stars, we came hoping to build something new and beautiful…"

Quantum brought up another display, a schedule. "It appears the Sun Smasher is on its way to *this* system for its next test operation. Based on current trajectory and system rotations, it should be here within three solar days."

She stood on the bridge as the behemoth *Star Sequencer 1* inexorably moved toward the next designated target. Just a short jump through the nearby Einstein-Rosen bridge was a small Undoc star system not unlike Sol, the origin point of all Earthmen, including Karen Reeves.

The ship was not terribly fast by modern standards, but it was massive with huge banks of energy-storage cells hidden within its armored flanks. This broad surface area allowed for the positioning of multiple gun emplacements, making the *SS1* as formidable as any U.P.C. Star Cav ship of the line. And for good reason: once fully-laden with the energy of three stars in its hold, the ship would be a prime target for Frontier outlaws and pirates.

Karen thrilled at the raw power enveloping her, a power manifested from her own will and vision. Once the *Star Sequencer 1* returned to Earth with a full payload, SuperCorp would hold a veritable monopoly on clean, affordable energy. The Unified Planetary Council would undoubtedly turn to SuperCorp for all its energy needs, and so her employer would gain preeminence in temporal and political power throughout the Civilized Systems. Karen would be a shoo-in to become the next CEO, where she would sit at the center of that expansive web of galactic power. The Master, or rather Mistress, of the Universe.

"Miss Reeves." The ship's captain, an older man named Kirby, stepped to her side, breaking Karen's reverie. "Forgive me, but we've just received an automated hail from the transport we dispatched to chase the Undoc ship escaping the Janglu test."

Karen frowned at the light-complexioned, middle-aged man. He was a carbon copy of so many of those who had opposed her on her climb up the corporate ladder. She wondered if, hidden behind that veneer of professional courtesy, Kirby did not secretly resent answering to her—a woman over a decade his junior. The thought gave her no small amount of joy.

"So? What is the problem?"

"The message is automated, as I said. The crew does not respond to our hails, claiming some technical problem with the communications equipment. This despite our network diagnostics showing no such problem."

Karen looked to the forward screen. "Backtrack the drive signature. Find out if and where it landed, then focus the long-range scanners on that location."

The captain relayed the order to an officer at the sensor terminal. After a few minutes, the report came back. "It appears to have landed on an inner world of our next target, the Kleppin system. Scans indicate a fairly sizeable Undoc settlement there. We've also picked up the presence of wreckage near the settlement. The signature matches the ship that escaped Janglu."

Karen rubbed her chin. "Have a company of troopers dispatched to the hangar bay with blast shielding, just in case it isn't our people aboard that transport. I want to be ready for anything."

Captain Kirby raised an eyebrow. "Wouldn't it be more prudent to destroy the ship before it lands if you suspect a possible threat to the project? If there's explosives aboard—"

Karen smiled. "There can't be enough to do more than cosmetic damage. And if there are Undocs and they put up a fight, then by all means, kill them. But transports and death benefits cost money, Captain. If something has happened to our crew, whatever is on that ship can provide the data I'll need for the quarter's profits and loss report."

The Sun Smasher was easily the largest manufactured thing the Warden had ever seen in space. Even the interdimensional battle cruisers of Quantum's people, the

Mechtechan, were dwarfed by the massive block of shining metal thrusting through the cosmos. Long and flat, and bristling with weapons batteries and sensor arrays, the SuperCorp monstrosity looked as if an insane god from some unimaginable afterlife had tossed a silver brick into reality.

"Quantum was right," the Warden growled. The plan—*his* plan—had already gone off the rails in a spectacular way. All because he wasn't yet up to speed on modern technology. Not that tech from his own time had ever been his strong suit.

The plan had entailed slipping aboard the Sun Smasher in the guise of the last surviving crewmember of the transport. He would feign injury, be escorted to sickbay, then sneak out and find a way to sabotage the massive star-devouring vessel from within. The Warden hadn't expected the SuperCorp communication network to require DNA identification to verify the user. As soon as he was forced to make use of the automated signal to respond to hails, he knew he was in trouble.

He realized just how much trouble when the titanic craft's tractor beam guided his stolen transport into one of the Sun Smasher's hangar bays. Via the ship's external cameras, he watched a full company of armored troopers take up firing positions behind mobile blast plates. With a sigh, he looked at the black corporate armor lying over the command chair beside him.

He briefly contemplated trying to pull on the gear and make a go of the original plan, but shook his head. "Quantum was right. I'm just glad he isn't here to know it."

The Warden's alien friend had wanted to accompany him despite his now validated criticisms of the plan. But in the end, they had decided it would be best for Quantum to remain with the *Ranger VII* and get it up and running, just in case the Warden needed a rescue from the approaching Sun Smasher.

What the Warden hadn't mentioned to Quantum was that he would never call for that rescue. With no ships of their own and no Star Cav ships nearby to signal for evacuation, the settlers had only one chance for survival: the Sun Smasher's destruction. And that chance, that responsibility, now rested squarely on the Warden's shoulders. He would succeed or die trying.

So, he surrendered.

Karen blinked at the trooper's announcement over the com. "Miss Reeves, we've captured the only person aboard the transport. We believe he's the man known on the Frontier as the Last Star Warden."

"Bring him to my office."

Karen sat back from her desk and laughed. The Last Star Warden? Ever since she'd come to the Frontier for the final phase of the project two months ago, she'd heard wild tales of the "Phantom Lawman," the "Ghost of the Frontier," and—most eloquent of the bunch—"The Specter of Sinister Space." She'd thought it was just so much folklore spun around card tables and barrooms by the down-and-out Undocs, bored spacers, and disgruntled wage slaves.

Shaking her head, Karen prepared to meet the preposterous prisoner. "I suppose it only feasible that such nonsense might inspire some idealistic fool to take up the mantle in an attempt at fame. He's probably just a glory-seeking moron, or simply insane."

A few moments later, four armored troopers escorted the idealistic fool into her ornately decorated office. Karen had to admit, if only to herself, that the man in the gravity shackles certainly looked the part. Taller than the average corporate desk-warrior, but not by much, his broad shoulders and athletic build were displayed by the blue and silver antique spacesuit he wore. The visored cowl of this form-fitting garment hid his features, save for his straight nose, high cheekbones, grim mouth, and square jaw.

One of the troopers handed Karen the prisoner's gun belt. She took note of the two elegant if primitive blaster pistols as well as the obscure logo on the silver buckle. Drawing one of the weapons, she tossed the rig onto the leather sofa beside the door.

"Who are you, and what have you done with my men?" She leveled the blaster's muzzle at the man. If she thought he'd show some response, she was disappointed.

"My name is not important." His voice was deep with a faint, familiar accent. "What matters is that I convince you to stop what you're doing aboard this ship. A great many lives are at stake, and so is the future."

Karen raised her chin. "The future of what? The Frontier? The handful of Undocs who have illegally claimed a miserable rock in an out-of-the-way system as their own?

And you still haven't answered my question about my men."

The Warden nodded. "They're dead. All of them. I gave them a chance, but I was not about to let them harm those settlers."

Karen turned and walked behind her desk, placed the ancient weapon on its glass surface. "That was a costly mistake. On my part. I would have let that little fellow from Janglu go if I'd known he would make straight for our next target. Now I'm in the red for eight security operators. But at least you brought my transport back. I suppose I should thank you for that, though these costs will be negligible once we've completed our tests."

The Warden's mouth hardened. "You don't understand. You're not just killing stars, you're killing whole systems, whole stretches of the galaxy. Eventually those black holes you're leaving behind will merge into a super hole, and all of the Frontier will die."

Karen narrowed her eyes. "So? There is nothing out here but death and desolation. The Tuatha Wars saw to that. Those alien monsters destroyed their own civilization rather than allow the U.P.C. to conquer them. They wiped themselves out and any chance we might have of ever colonizing this part of space in a dozen lifetimes."

"That isn't all that long in the grand scheme of things, believe me. And these Undocs you're talking about are doing it. They are actually making a viable living on these so-called desolate worlds. In a few generations, they will be the ones who will have made it possible for the Frontier to become part of the Civilized Worlds. And your Sun Smasher is destroying that possibility, that future."

Karen sneered. "All those Undocs are doing is killing themselves and their children slowly. What right have they to come out here and defy the laws of the U.P.C.? They should be back where they belong, in the Civilized Worlds, earning wages, paying bills, and buying merchandise to finance real innovation and exploration. What gives them the right to rebel against a system that has made Earth the economic center of the galaxy for centuries?"

The Warden tilted his head as if he were speaking to a child, annoying Karen to no end. "They're people, just like you and me. That alone gives them every right in the world."

"Get him out of here. Put him in a holding cell until I decide what to do with him."

Alone in the office, she picked up the blaster and shoved it back into its holster. She traced the etched logo on the belt buckle. A single world silhouetted against a bright star, the planet's orbit a silver ellipse balanced against six golden rays of the sunburst.

"The Last Star Warden, huh?"

The Warden paced his holding cell for over an hour before she came. He waited as she dismissed the guards. She was not wearing the smart business suit she'd worn in the office. Her new attire looked something like an evening gown made of stars and distant galaxies, sparkling like her dark eyes. Her raven hair was freed from the severe bun she'd sported earlier, the thick tresses cascading over her toned shoulders.

"Miss... I'm sorry. I didn't get your name."

She smiled, playfully now, not mean or angry. "And I still don't know yours, Warden."

"That's good enough for me. So, do I call you Miss President, Miss CEO, or something else?"

She laughed. It was a pleasant sound. "I am Karen Reeves, Senior VP in charge of Research and Development for SuperCorp. But Karen will suffice."

"Well, Miss Reeves," the Warden said. "Are you going to a party? Or do you always get dolled up before sentencing your prisoners?"

"You intrigue me, Warden. Not many men do. Most of them are so obvious, so clumsy in their attempts at getting what they want. So desperate to gain approval, to be told they are good little boys. So afraid of failing, but more afraid of actually succeeding."

"Sounds like you've mistaken something else for men."

Her smile widened. "Where do you come from, Warden? Not Earth, surely. A lost colony on the Frontier perhaps, isolated by the Tuatha Wars and the subsequent Frontier Preservation Acts? Somewhere that builds *real* men and not the simpering, obsequious, milquetoast specimens we now have in the Civilized Worlds?"

The Warden took a deep breath. "I'm from Earth. A small town that's probably not even there anymore."

She frowned, trying to remember something. "Your accent... Are you from the North American Collective?"

The Warden shrugged. In his day, it had still been called the United States of America. In any case, his origins, now lost to time, were no business of hers. "So, are you going to tell me why you're here? Why we're alone and why you're dressed like that?"

She ran a hand slowly along his upper arm, her long-lashed eyes looking him up and down. "I could use a man like you out here, Warden. A man with the skill to take down eight troopers singlehandedly and the gall to try and sneak aboard this ship alone... well, such a man could demand a very *handsome* price for his... services."

The Warden didn't have to stretch his imagination to understand her double meaning. "I don't fight for money, and I certainly don't do the other for it, either. Peddle your wares somewhere else, Miss Reeves, 'cause I ain't buying."

She stiffened, her nostrils flaring. "I thought you were a bit slow, Warden, but I didn't suspect you were downright stupid. Don't you realize I could have you killed with a word?"

He nodded. "Just like the word you gave to kill those Undocs on Janglu. Just like the word that will kill the settlers on Kleppin 3. The difference is, you've actually seen me, spoken to me. I'm real to you now, and that reality will haunt you for the rest of your life if you kill me. And then you'll start to feel the weight of all the other souls you've consigned to eternity with your *words*. That weight will crush you, destroy you in the end, Miss Reeves."

She spun to face the wall, her hands knotting into shaking fists. "I hate the Undocs," she said in a low, husky voice. "I'd kill them all if I could. Lousy, grubby, murdering bastards."

The Warden raised his chin in sudden understanding. He stared at her quivering back and said in a low voice, "The Breakthrough. I've heard about it. You were there?"

Reeves turned and faced him, her chin set defiantly. No tears marred her cheeks, but her dark eyes glistened in the fluorescent light. "Twenty-five years ago, when the Star Cav blockade first tried to seal off the Frontier at the end of the Tuatha Wars. My parents were officers aboard the *Falk-Moore*, one of the battleships in the blockade.

"The fighting had been over for several months. No one thought there was any danger, no one thought to evacuate the non-combatants from the warships. No one expected an entire armada of Undoc blockade runners to launch a suicide attack in their mad dash for the Frontier. Two thousand civilian ships pitted against sixty-four U.P.C. warships. To this day, no one knows how many of the bastards got through…"

She touched a glimmer at the edge of her left eye and sniffed. "I was one of twenty-two survivors aboard the *Falk-Moore*, found by rescue crews four days after the battle. I don't know if I dreamed it, or if it was real… but at some point, in those four days, I saw my mother's frozen corpse drift by the porthole of my sealed compartment…

"So, believe me, Warden, I'll not shed a single tear nor lose a single moment's sleep for the death of any number of those Undoc scum."

The Warden shook his head. "I'm sorry for your loss. But there are children on Kleppin 3, children who will suffer just as you suffered aboard your parents' ship. And if one of them survives, he or she might be filled with that same kind of hatred, and in twenty-five years, we could be facing another Breakthrough, or something even worse. You have a chance to end the cycle here and now."

She laughed bitterly. "Well then, I guess we'll just have to make sure no one escapes this time." She turned to the door and shouted, "Guards!"

"Please," the Warden said. "Yours is the power to give life and peace. That is an awesome responsibility and a very precious gift. Please, don't squander it."

Reeves sneered as she told the guards, "Take him to the nearest airlock and space him."

The armored men grabbed the Warden and hauled him from the cell. Reeves said, "I'll be looking out my office window, Warden, watching for your frozen corpse."

When the four troopers crowded him into a service lift, the Warden said, "You guys realize this is wrong, don't you? This has got to stop before anyone else gets hurt or killed."

One of the men drove the butt of his blaster carbine into the Warden's ribs, still sore from his tussle with the pirates. "Shut up, weirdo."

Wincing at the pain, the Warden took a deep breath. "Look, this doesn't have to end bloody. If you help me, we can take over this ship without a struggle—"

"I said shut up!" The trooper swung the weapon again, but the Warden moved.

His hands were bound by the gravity shackles in front of him and he was surrounded by four armed and armored mercenaries. But the Warden's head and feet were still free. In the tight confines of the elevator, it was not a fair fight at all.

When the lift reached the airlock level, the Warden stepped from the smoke-filled car. The four unconscious guards lay on the floor along with the gravity shackles. The Warden held a blaster carbine in each of his freed hands.

Scanning the floorplan layout beneath the elevator's keypad, he devised the quickest route to the ship's command center. Then he went to work.

"He's taken the bridge," Captain Kirby announced over the com. "He incapacitated the posted guards and forced the command crew out at gunpoint. I'm sorry, Miss Reeves, there's nothing we could do."

Karen rubbed the bridge of her nose and took a deep breath. She would see Kirby ruined for this, but right now she had to solve the bigger problem. "I want every able-bodied trooper armed and ready for a full assault on the bridge in two minutes. Issue sidearms to everyone else and have them stand in reserve. In the meantime, you and the bridge crew meet me at the auxiliary command center."

"Ah…" There was a staticky pause on the other end of the channel.

"What is it, Captain?"

"Well, Miss Reeves, I'm afraid the auxiliary command center is not fully operational. It was not deemed necessary for the initial tests."

Karen slammed her fist onto the glass-topped desk. She'd find out who had made that decision and have them join Kirby in the unemployment line. "Well, get a crew down there and see what functions *can* be commandeered. Immediately!"

Karen ended the call and headed for her quarters. The crisis at hand required something much more functional than her best evening gown.

The com chirped. It was a ship-wide announcement. "This is the Star Warden. I have taken control of this ship. I will be powering down the engines and contacting the nearest Star Cav flotilla, informing them of the illegal nature of this craft's function and operation. I advise all crewmembers to return to your quarters and await the arrival of duly-appointed officials. There is no need to further involve yourselves in the crimes of your superiors. That is all."

Karen glared at the speaker. "The hell it is."

"I wish Quantum was here," the Warden growled. Despite his announcement, he found himself unable to operate the controls of the titanic spaceship. Just like the communications array on the transport, the bridge controls were DNA locked. Only now did the Warden realize that whatever Quantum had done to the transport had allowed him to even get it off the ground in the first place.

The only reason he had access to the coms was the system was still running when he'd taken the bridge. The other stations' operators had had enough time to shut their systems down.

"I'm over a hundred years behind the tech curve," the Warden sighed. "I should have kept a crewmember just to use his thumbprint."

A blazing light along the edge of the sealed blast door caught his attention. He scanned the security terminals and saw the outer corridor filled with armored troopers.

They used a plasma torch to cut their way into the bridge.

The Warden picked up the two blaster carbines and stepped behind a command station. He wasn't sure how many charges each of the newer weapons carried, but he knew whatever that payload was, that was the number of mercenaries about to wind up in the loss column of SuperCorp's ledgers.

"Unless there's a better way." He looked at the control panels one more time.

Karen stormed into the auxiliary command center with four troopers in tow, a blaster pistol strapped to her thigh. She wore a tailored version of the gray corporate jumpsuit issued to all members of the crew. "Captain Kirby, what is the current situation?"

The older man frowned, looked up from a console where a pair of junior officers frantically tapped out code. A trio of mechanics and engineers hurried to impart functionality to useless equipment under the other two consoles in the small room. "We've got communications, so there's no need to worry about our guest calling the authorities. We should have helm control within the next ten minutes."

"What about engineering? He still hasn't cut power to the engines."

"Working on it. Apparently, this Star Warden hasn't been able to do much of anything since taking the bridge. The security teams are about to breach, so the situation may well be resolved before we're finished down here."

Karen thought about the man who had rejected her, the man who had challenged her to do *the right thing* while facing certain death. She shook her head. "I doubt that very seriously, Captain. Keep at it."

A low moan thrummed through the ship. Karen felt a pit open in her stomach, as though she had just fallen a considerable distance. "What is that?"

Kirby looked at the control panel. "I... I don't know how, but he's caused the ship to accelerate to maximum speed. Beyond normal safety protocols."

"Why would he do that?"

Kirby looked disturbed. "No idea. Our current rate of acceleration and trajectory will carry us *into* the Kleppin star within the next two hours. That is *if* we don't shake apart first."

Karen tapped one of the officers at the terminal on the shoulder. "Get me helm controls right now!"

The young woman looked up as her screen went black. "I'm sorry, Miss Reeves. *All* helm controls just went down. So did a lot of other systems. The entire command network needs to be rebooted."

Karen looked up at the white star in the view screen as it grew larger and larger with each passing second. "We've got to get to engineering and shut down those engines."

As she turned to go, a voice boomed across the ship-wide intercom. The shouted sentences were punctuated by the sounds of blaster fire and distant cries of pain:

"This is the Star Warden... Sorry things didn't work out as planned... but it looks like this ship is headed for a collision course with the nearest star... I highly recommend everyone get to a transport or a lifeboat and get off this thing as soon as possible... That is all."

The junior officers stared at her, then looked at Kirby. They jumped to their feet and led the technicians from the room in a hurry.

"Stop! I'll have you all fired!" Karen shouted after them. She turned to her security detail. "Shoot them!" But the armored men were already following the crewmembers to safety.

Karen drew her blaster pistol.

"Miss Reeves!" Captain Kirby said. "Please, you must be reasonable."

Karen leveled the pistol at him. "How long to shut down the engines once we get to engineering?"

Kirby stood straight and shook his head. "I'm afraid it is out of the question. We may shut the engines down, but without control of the retrorockets, our current momentum will still carry us into the star's corona long before we can reboot the system. I'm afraid we've lost."

Karen shot him.

The captain fell to the floor, his pale eyes showing more disappointment than surprise or even anger. Karen had anger enough for both of them as she watched the man die. "That is but one of the many differences between the two of us, Kirby. I never lose."

Holstering the weapon, Karen ran from the small room, headed for engineering.

The Warden crouched behind the smoking control terminal. He had yanked as many wires and cables from under the helm console as he could before the troopers had breached the room. Only his hurried announcement of the ship's pending destruction had quelled the onslaught of armored men onto the bridge.

And none too soon. Both of his captured weapons were out of ammo. A score of corporate grunts scattered around the haze-filled room attested to the efficient use of that ammunition.

Rising from behind cover, the Warden realized he was alone on the bridge. As soon as one trooper had made the decision to save himself rather than face the meat-grinder in the control room, the rout had begun. Mercenaries could only be counted on to fight so long as they held the upper hand. Most men's loyalty to a paycheck came up short somewhere before possible death or dismemberment.

The Warden scanned the few controls still operational and concluded that he had no chance of preventing the Sun Smasher from colliding with the Kleppin star. At least not without the aid of someone with access to the controls. Just as the security guards had fled, he was certain all noncombatant SuperCorp crewmembers would be boarding escape craft with as much alacrity as they could muster.

There was only one person who might still be willing to save this ship. The Warden snatched up another rifle from the floor and ran from the smoke-filled bridge. "If I can just convince her this time."

Surprisingly, he met very little resistance on his way to Reeves's office—just a few desperate pot-shots fired by fleeing troopers or scared crewmembers. Unsurprisingly, the senior vice president was not there as the Warden had hoped. Still, he was able to recover his Comets.

As he buckled on the gun belt, Karen Reeves's voice came through the ship's intercom. "If anyone is still listening, I want you to know that your performance reviews will reflect your negative behavior on this project, and I will be recommending disciplinary action in the form of punitive fines for the lot of you.

"As for you, Star Warden... I want you to know you haven't won. I've activated the siphoning drive. The Kleppin star may kill the *SS1*, but it will be a pyrrhic victory, and all your precious little Undocs will live out the remainder of their limited days on a freezing planet in the dwindling glow of a dying star."

The Warden lowered his head and took a deep breath. He hadn't counted on Reeves's hatred driving her to this. Leaving the office, he grabbed the first crewmember he saw and demanded directions to the siphoning drive control room.

Karen eased into the command chair of her private shuttle and flicked on the communication monitor, linking it directly to the siphoning control room. She was not disappointed. By the time her tiny ship had powered up and begun its departure protocols, she saw the Star Warden run into the empty room on the *SS1*.

"There you are," she said, smiling. She knew her value to SuperCorp would be devastated by this debacle. She would at least have the small satisfaction of watching the man responsible for it die. "I knew you'd make it."

The Warden scanned the room for an instant before replying. "You don't have to do this, Miss Reeves. Tell me how to shut this thing down, and you can save thousands of lives. You can be the savior of entire worlds."

She laughed, remembering a history lesson from long ago. "What was it Oppenheimer said when humanity first harnessed the power of the atom? 'Now I am become Death, the destroyer of worlds.' Well, I, Karen Fran Reeves, have trumped him. I am the destroyer of entire star systems.

"And apparently I have accomplished what no one has been able to do for over a hundred years: I have also destroyed the last of the Star Wardens."

The Warden spared her a crooked smile as his head swiveled, taking in the massive banks of controls and generators that were coming to life. She watched the room fill with an electric blue glow as the siphoning engines acquired full power.

The Warden looked out of the monitor as if she were there, face to face.

"I've gotten out of worse," he said before blasting the camera and robbing her of her final victory.

She cursed and jerked at the controls as her shuttle left the titanic *Star Sequencer 1.* The action caused one of the craft's wings to clip an antenna array. The shuttle spiraled out of control, and Karen was hurled from her chair.

In the haste to savor her revenge, she had not buckled in.

The Warden stood at the control panel, trying to make sense of the power levels and range figures scrolling across the screen. He pushed several buttons, knowing he would get the flashing red "User Not Recognized" response. He picked up the SuperCorp carbine and headed into the workings of the star siphoning engine.

"I may not know how to access this modern technology, but I still know how to gum up a machine."

The chamber was enormous, at least as big as the orbital shipyard facility that had built the Ranger-class ships back in his day. A ship-sized cylinder running through the middle of the chamber, supported by struts and buttresses connecting to the surrounding walls, occupied most of this cavernous space. Massive banks of cooling units ran along this gargantuan tube at regular intervals, indicating the inordinate amount of heat the device would generate. And it indicated the Achilles' heel of the entire setup.

The Warden blasted the first of these cooling units into Freon-spraying scrap.

Alarms turned the blue-infused room red and filled the entire chamber with a deafening clarion when the unit went up in smoke. The Warden blasted more coolant systems. But the siphoning engine continued to power up. Reeves had apparently countermanded any fail-safes the engineers may have put in place.

Coughing against the poisonous gas slowly filling the chamber, the Warden continued his endless and hopeless battle against the enormous sun-destroying machine's cooling units. A hundred meters into the tunnel surrounding the device, he spotted a possible weak link. The siphoning engine narrowed like the pinch point in an hourglass before widening again to colossal proportions. This pinch point was about the size of a stateroom on a vacation liner, but the Warden reasoned it would be the easiest portion of the behemoth to damage.

He raised the carbine and pulled the trigger.

The weapon made a dry click. It was empty.

The machine began to hum, filling the entire chamber with sound as well as a nauseating heat. Within seconds, sweat covered the Warden and he could barely catch his breath.

Dropping the SuperCorp blaster, he drew his Comets and opened fire on the bottleneck chamber. It exploded on the second shot.

The Warden sailed through the burning, poisonous air. He slammed hard into a bulkhead, reigniting the agony in his ribs. The pain cleared his thoughts. Taking advantage of the dwindling gravity, he propelled himself down the shaft to the control room—just ahead of the conflagration filling the tunnel surrounding the siphoning engine.

Singed and gasping for breath, the Warden's tear-blurred vision fell on the emergency airlock. He dived through the blast door and sealed it. A second later, flame consumed the control room. Snatching a GlasSteel helmet and oxygen pack from the wall, he donned the gear and hit the airlock release.

Surrounded by crushing silence, the Star Warden was flushed into open space. Though the violence of his ejection carried him almost a kilometer away from the dying Sun Smasher, the ship filled his vision. From his perspective, the ship seemed larger than the moons surrounding Kleppin 3, even larger than the Undoc world itself.

This illusion lasted for several minutes before the massive ship's velocity carried it deeper into the system. And though the Warden knew an inferno raged within the leviathan's belly, no visible sign shone along its outer hull. The Sun Smasher seemed wholly intact right up to the moment it entered the star's corona. Any explosion on the ship was obscured by the sun's brightness.

The Star Warden took a deep breath and let everything settle in as he hung suspended in open space. He had succeeded in saving Kleppin 3 and the families now calling it home, but he had failed to save Karen Reeves from the hatred that had consumed and twisted her.

He touched the com on his wrist chrono. "Quantum, can you hear me?"

"Good to know you are still among the living." His friend's voice was staticky but audible. "Watching that ship come into this system caused an almost religious fervor among the locals. I thought you might become the first martyr of this nascent faith."

The Warden smiled. "So everything's okay down there?"

"As far as I can tell. We do have a new visitor. A SuperCorp shuttle crash-landed nearby. The only occupant, a human woman of some apparent importance was badly injured. But the Halums have taken her in and are tending her wounds along with the pilot of the first crash."

The Warden's smile widened. "Who knows? Maybe Frontier hospitality will prevail where Frontier justice failed."

"Meaning?"

"Never mind. Just come and get me if it's not too much of an inconvenience. It's been a long day."

The Haunted Station

The Last Star Warden stared into the infinite beauty of the cosmos, wondering if in all that limitless space there might be a way to get back to his own time. The longer he remained in this new era, he found it harder and harder to stare into the void without feeling a growing sense of soul-numbing loneliness. He did not like this new sensation, as his entire life had been spent looking to the stars and finding nothing but hope and inspiration.

He sat at the helm of the *Ranger VII*, guiding the silvery sleek deep-patrol ship farther into the wild reaches of Frontier Space. Though the Star Wardens had ceased to exist decades before, he continued their mission of maintaining the peace, the mission for which he had been trained. It was the only thing he knew how to do. It was the only thing that made sense to him in this modern, morally ambiguous era. The mission was his purpose.

The mission was his identity.

An automated distress signal sounded over the coms. "*To any ship within range, this is CRS-T33 in the HPL-37 system. We need your help. Please respond as soon as possible... To any ship...*"

"Quantum," the Warden called down to the crew compartment. "Looks like someone out there needs our help."

"Someone always does." The tall, slender blue alien climbed onto the bridge, his short antennae flicking atop his elongated skull. His oversized black eyes rarely blinked, and his small mouth seemed forever locked in a patronizing grin, as if silently judging this dimension.

Like the Warden, Quantum was a veteran of the Continuum War that had raged but for a few horrific weeks over a hundred years ago. A war waged between the Mechtechan, Quantum's own interdimensional race of conquerors, and the Star Wardens, the United Planetary Council's first deep-space security agency. That war had saved this plane of existence from the Mechtechan at great cost. It had also hurled the Warden and Quantum out of their own time and space, placing them in an unlikely partnership which had grown into genuine friendship over the past several months.

The Warden gave a square-jawed smile. "It's not like we have anything better to do." He set a course for the signal's origin. "Whoever is in trouble is way out on their own. The system doesn't even have a name, just a designation: HPL-37. I don't think too many Undocs have made it this far yet, and I doubt if any Star Cav patrols come this way very often."

"I would surmise smugglers or pirates, then." Quantum slipped into the navigator's chair. "Or perhaps another rogue corporate experiment? Most likely a trap of some sort."

The Warden frowned at that thought. "Let's hope not."

Within a few hours, the *Ranger VII*'s three atomic engines carried the Warden and Quantum through the nearest Einstein-Rosen bridge. Passing through the controlled wormhole network, they emerged into the isolated HPL-37 system at the extreme edge of the Milky Way's core. It was a desolate system, to be sure. Two barren, moonless worlds orbiting a white dwarf. A perpetual dust shroud from a long-disintegrated comet hung over the system like heavy fog. Apart from the communication buoys and the ERB at the system's edge, there was very little else.

Or so it first appeared.

"Look." Quantum pulled up an image and magnified it on the visual display. "There, hidden in the shadow of the inner world, almost invisible to scans. A space station."

The foreboding structure loomed above the planet, looking like nothing so much as a gothic tower ripped from some ancient fortification and hurled into the firmament by a terrible and demonic force. The long, black cylinder of CRS-T 33 bristled with barbed antennae and sensor arrays, as well as a handful of railguns and rocket batteries as it slowly twisted in its orbit. A fitful electric light from within its darkened portholes flashed in places along its outer hull.

The Warden nodded. "Whoever is on that thing didn't want any casual observers to notice them. Or to be pestered if they were. Let's hail them and see what's what."

There was no response to the hail, only the continued automated request for help.

"There is something wrong with our long-range sensors," Quantum said. "Readouts are fluctuating between one and fifty-nine lifeforms on that station. The irregular readings must be caused by a multi-spectrum interference. There appears to be some form of energy distortion surrounding the station, but I cannot identify it yet."

"Well, we are using salvaged parts on a ship that was technically obsolete some seventy or eighty years ago... I'll take us closer."

"The station's automated defense systems are locking onto us." There was no emotion in Quantum's observation. "They are powering up to fire."

The Warden shrugged. "I don't know if this'll work, but it's worth a shot." He sent a Star Warden jurisdictional authorization code to the station. "Who knows how old this thing is?"

Quantum's large, childlike eyes narrowed. "It appears to have worked. This is far newer technology than was used by your people in the time of our war. However, from what I have gathered, the U.P.C.'s advancements have moved at such a rapid pace that they simply overwrite the older systems rather than deleting them. I surmise that your access codes are still buried deep in this facility's operating systems."

"Well, at least we've got that much going for us. What about those energy distortions? Dangerous?"

"Negative. Most of the power seems to be contained within the facility. I am detecting nothing that would be harmful to your biology as far as radiation is concerned."

Docking the *Ranger VII* to the station, the Warden pulled his suit's skullcap over his head so that the black HUD visor concealed the upper half of his face. "Then let's see if we can get to the bottom of this mystery."

Quantum said, "If we can trust our sensors at all, the energy distortion does not seem to be affecting the radiant temperature. As if the energy is going somewhere… else. Strange."

The Warden and Quantum donned their GlasSteel helmets and oxygen tanks. As always, the Warden wore his twin Comet blasters, and Quantum carried his long particle-beam rifle. There were too many questions surrounding the station not to play it safe. Who had built the isolated and remote station, and why? What had befallen the facility to necessitate a distress signal? What was the source of the strange energy, and where was it going? Possibly of more importance, what were the station's uncommunicative crew—or whoever was on the thing—willing to do to keep it secret?

Passing through the airlock and into the station, the Warden recognized the interior design. The rectangular walls and horizontal walkways with a clearly defined sense of up-and-down, along with the word-symbols emblazoned on emergency and control panels, were the telltale earmarks of human construction. "Definitely built by folks from the Sol system."

Flickering overhead florescent panels lit the corridor leading away from the airlock, though the far end faded into darkness. A low, creaking groan thrummed mechanically through the metal walls and deck plating.

Quantum stepped to a control panel beside the sealed airlock. "According to this readout, atmospherics are at optimal level. Artificial gravity is set to Earthman standards. As I suspected, no indication of toxins or other biohazards."

"Okay. Looks like we can shed the helmets and Ox."

Only a few steps down the corridor, the overhead light panels went completely dark. Before the Warden could change the spectrum of his visor, a low, mournful wail echoed from somewhere deep inside the station. The voice sent a cold chill creeping up his spine.

"Did you hear that?" The Warden turned to Quantum as his visor switched to night vision. "Sounded like someone in pain."

"Or someone dying." In tones of emerald and jade, his friend's face was even less expressive than usual. "We should be careful."

"Come on." The Warden headed to the end of the corridor. The automated door opened at their approach. "Well, at least not everything is out of order."

They stepped into another corridor, this one much wider with gently sloping walls to indicate a spiraling, circular path. It was also fully lit.

Switching back to normal vision, the Warden noted other doors lining this central hallway. There was an unsettling stillness, something akin to the sensation of entering a large and unfamiliar building and knowing with absolute certainty that no other living being is anywhere inside it.

A grey toolbox lay overturned on the deck, spilled wrenches and drivers scattered on the rubberized floor. Shards of broken fluorescent bulbs surrounded it. The Warden knelt to look at these, then turned to the door through which they had come. He rubbed his chin. "Someone was on their way to repair the lights in that corridor when… something happened."

"But what?" Quantum scanned the immediate surroundings. "Other than this disarray, I see no sign of a struggle. No biological tissue, no scuff marks. Nothing."

The Warden looked in both directions of the circular corridor, noting the security cameras set in the ceiling panels. "Let's look for the command center. I'm sure we'll find some answers there."

As they set off to the right, that disquieting moan sounded from somewhere on a deck high above them. A moment or two after its last echo had faded, it was answered by a fearsome shriek far below.

The *Magpie 6* emerged from the comet fog, a hunched, rugged ship built to survive the dangers of asteroid-belt mining and Sargasso salvage operations. It had once been painted a rich scarlet and gold, but now looked to be covered in rust. Only the blue fire of its fusion drive and amber running lights gave it the impression of modern technology. It did not glide through space so much as crawled over it.

"Is that a Ranger-class ship?" Ramirez touched the display screen, magnifying the silver craft docked with the darkened station. Looking up from the image, she asked, "How old is this place, Rook?"

Rook, the salvage ship's captain, shook his head. "Not that old." Rubbing the stubble on his chin, he looked at the antique ship. "Looks like somebody beat us to the party…"

Ramirez, the first mate, pulled her long dark curls back and looped them into a tail. "You don't think it could really be… *him*, do you? I didn't think…"

"The Phantom Lawman?" Rook scoffed, returned to his command chair. "You know anybody else flying a mint-condition Ranger in the Frontier? This complicates things… Send the access code and initiate docking procedures."

Taking his seat, Rook flipped the intercom switch and announced to his crew, "All right boys and girls, we've got a hot date with some prime salvage. There may be some legal entanglements, so let's play nice for the time being. Suit up and prepare to board."

Ramirez didn't look up from her task at the helm. "You think we might have to get physical?"

Rook shifted his massive frame in the command chair. "If my tip was right, what's down there is worth more than the net worth of some planets. So, if it comes to it, yeah, I mean to get physical, 'Ghost of the Frontier' or no. Besides, it's high time Strega earned his pay."

"All shuttles and escape pods are present and accounted for." Quantum's three-fingered hands moved across the console, flipping through displays. "With the exception of the heightened energy readings and the ensuing power surges, most everything on the station appears to be fully operational."

The Warden and Quantum stood in the station's command center, surrounded by computer terminals, 3D charts, system displays, and rectangular windows showing a panoramic view of the fog-enshrouded system. The overhead lighting flickered every time the decks and bulkheads creaked with a strange rattling noise.

"And the crew? Are the station's sensors picking them up?"

Quantum shook his head. "No. The copious energy output is interfering with the internal sensors. Based on this personnel report, there should be fifty-nine people aboard."

"Can you isolate the location of that energy output?"

Quantum flipped through a few more displays. "The lowest tier appears to be a sealed radiation-proof chamber used for energy experiments. I propose that to be the source."

Another disembodied wail sounded from just outside the command center.

The Warden checked the security monitors. There was nothing in the outer corridor, just like there was nothing in every other part of the station. At least according to the cameras. Unable to shake the uneasy feeling he'd had since first boarding the station, he asked, "What about the logs? Anything to explain where everybody went?"

Quantum looked up from the console. "It would appear the logs are kept on a secure server in a different location. The operations of this facility are highly compartmentalized, indicating that its purpose was of a high-security and clandestine nature. However, by analyzing the information I have here, I would surmise that this was a science and research center."

"But researching what? And who was doing the research? From what I can tell, there are components on this ship from several different corporations. Could this be a U.P.C. black ops facility? If so, there might be a Star Cav warship on its way in response to that distress signal. We might not want to be here when it arrives."

An automated proximity alert sounded from one of the consoles: "*Ship approaching at intercept trajectory. Slowing to docking velocity.*"

The Warden stepped to the window, spotting the approaching ship. "Looks like we've got company. If they're Star Cav or a U.P.C. envoy, maybe they've got some answers."

Quantum scanned the ship. "Highly unlikely. Though they are submitting the proper access codes, the ship's registration indicates that it is a salvage vessel based in Centauri Prime. They have come for an easy score, no doubt."

The Warden rested his hands on the butts of his Comet blasters, wondering how a salvager out of Centauri Prime had the station's access codes. Or even knew the station was here, for that matter. "Not 'til we get to the bottom of this. Let's go welcome them aboard and make sure they understand that."

Rook stood in the airlock with Ramirez and the rest of his crew. Brock, the blonde Undoc engineer he'd picked up on that rundown station in Orion's Belt, stood beside her two assistants, the shifty-eyed Hicks and the goateed Chan. Rook's resident bruiser, the hulking, saurian alien Strega, occupied almost as much space as the rest of the crew. The humans wore boarding armor and carried sidearms and shotguns or submachineguns. Strega wore his vibro-ax strapped across his broad, scaly back. The saurian didn't need armor, his hide being impervious to all but heavy blaster fire.

"You think we'll need all this hardware?" Ramirez asked quietly as the chamber's pressure equalized with that of the station. "Maybe we should leave somebody on the ship."

"The payday promised by this place demands we put all our pieces on the board. Even if it didn't, *his* presence would." Rook shook his head as the first door opened. He could see two figures dimly outlined behind the GlasSteel barrier of the next chamber. "I've heard some stories about this guy. If only half of 'em are true, I don't want to take any chances."

When the final portal opened, Rook led his crew into the corridor to face the man and blue alien waiting to greet them. The Last Star Warden was slightly shorter than Rook, but not as bulky. The alien was taller and thinner still. Both wore old-fashioned form-fitting blue and silver spacesuits. The man's entailed a skull-cap and visor, which concealed most of his face.

Both were armed.

"Rook, captain of the *Magpie 6*, and crew. Requesting permission to come aboard."

The man surveyed the group, obviously taking note of their martial gear. The hint of a smile played at the edge of his grim mouth. "You can call me Warden. And this is Quantum. What's the nature of your business here, Captain Rook?"

"We were looking for hulks to salvage from the Tuatha Wars in the next system over and heard the distress signal. Came to see if we could lend a hand."

"How did you come by the access codes for this place? If you don't mind me asking."

Rook smiled. The man was shrewd. "We've got a database of all kinds of access codes. Comes in handy in our line of work... Look, do you want our help or not?"

The Warden kept his hands resting on the hilts of his belted guns. "Maybe... We just got here ourselves and haven't yet been able to locate any of the station's crew. If we work together, we should be able to search this place up and down and find out what happened."

Rook smiled wider. "Happy to oblige, Warden. However, before we get started, I'd like to invoke the Right of Salvage as outlined in Star Law 19-39.12a. If we don't find anybody aboard, then we are entitled to any and all resources on the abandoned vessel. Naturally, seeing as how you two got here first, we'd be willing to negotiate a finder's fee." He looked pointedly at the Warden's guns. "A generous one, of course."

The Warden's hinted smile turned instantly to a frown. "We can discuss salvaging issues later, Captain. As a duly appointed Officer of the Law, and in accordance with Star Law 3-42.1, I am declaring this an active crime scene until further notice. Now, do you want to help or not?"

Rook heard Strega hiss behind him, felt the tension from his crew. "Like I said, we're here to help, first and foremost. Where do we start?"

An unholy shriek tore through the station's intercom system.

The Warden tilted his head. "How 'bout we begin by looking for whoever's doing that?"

"We should split up and cover more ground," Rook suggested as they entered the station's central winding corridor.

The Warden nodded. He didn't trust the big scavenger as far as he could throw him in super gravity, but in this the newcomer had a point. "All right, you and half your crew come with me to search the lower decks. The rest go with Quantum to the upper. We've already checked the control room, but there's no logs indicating what happened here. My guess is the head of the facility will have a private system with that info on it, either in quarters or an office."

"What about the energy output?" The question came from the wiry blonde woman in Rook's crew. She wore tool pouches as well as ammo bandoliers on her web gear. "Have you located the source? I'm an engineer, maybe I should look into that."

The Warden shrugged. "Our first priority, for now, is to locate the station's crew. Or at least find out what happened to them. Go with Quantum; he may need your help breaking into the administrator's system."

He knew his friend would require no such help, but he was not about to let a scavenger poke around something that could be responsible for the entire weird scenario. At least not until they had more information.

Rook nodded. "He's right, Brock. You take Chan and Hickman with… Quantum. Me, Ramirez, and Strega will go with the Warden."

Another shriek and moan echoed from somewhere in the station. The decks creaked eerily in the ensuing silence.

"Did you see that?" Rook's brunette first mate, Ramirez, raised the muzzle of her submachinegun in the direction of the right corridor. "Something moved down there."

The saurian alien, Strega, lifted his head and tasted the air with a glowing purple tongue. "Human. Sssoiled. Male."

The Warden headed that way. "Come on. Keep the coms channels open and report anything you find."

He reached a four-way intersection ahead of Rook and his team. The central corridor crossed a narrower hall leading to storage lockers to the right and a stairwell to the left. Trusting that Strega's assessment was true, the Warden touched his visor to see ambient thermal temperatures, hoping to track the individual by his heat signature.

He caught a whiff of body odor and filth. Something hit him. Hard. The attack knocked the wind from his lungs. Strong, feral hands scratched and clawed at him.

The Warden's spacesuit kept the fiend's ragged nails from finding purchase in his flesh as they went to the floor. Rolling with the impact, the Warden took advantage of his screaming, snarling assailant's momentum.

The manic individual sailed through the air to slam against the far bulkhead.

The Warden rose to one knee as Rook and his crewmates arrived on scene, weapons drawn. His attacker was a scrawny man in a tattered and grimy grey jumpsuit. Cowering on the deck, the man's dark hair was shaggy and unkempt, his face covered in dirt and several days' worth of stubble. His brown eyes were wide and full of madness as he whimpered, "Please... please don't take me to hell... Please don't make me a ghost... Please..."

Rook laughed, holstering his blaster pistol. "Looks like you won't be getting much from this one, Warden. He's loopier than a Senesian moon's orbit."

The Warden dusted off his shoulders. "Looks like you won't be salvaging this place, Rook. It's not abandoned after all."

The captain's laugh died as his face went hard. The big saurian hissed, bony ridges along the top of his skull extending menacingly, his green scales taking on a reddish hue. Only the woman, Ramirez, showed no sign of frustration.

She looked at the cowering man with a mixture of pity and fear. "What happened here?"

Rook motioned to the alien hulk. "That's what we're going to find out. Strega, grab him. Take him to our ship's med bay and try to calm him down enough to talk."

The Warden stepped between the mad crewman and the saurian bruiser. "No. I'll take him and see if we can find the station's medical facilities. Besides, there may be records there that could give us some clues. You three keep looking for more crewmembers."

Strega's clawed hands flexed into scaly fists and his yellow eyes dilated. One eye swiveled, looking to Rook for an order.

The Warden didn't move.

"Fine." The scavenger captain's face slid into his wolfish grin. "But take Ramirez with you, Warden. She can watch your back in case there's any more of these nut-jobs running loose. Hate for you to get *outnumbered* and taken down."

The Warden returned the smile. "Thanks for your concern, but I'm pretty sure I can take care of myself."

Rook motioned Strega to follow him down the storage corridor. "I'm sure you can. Still, misery loves company. Ramirez, you're with the Warden."

When they reached the first storage bay, Rook did not bother to attempt the lock. Making sure the Warden was watching, he signaled Strega to use the big vibro-ax. The saurian alien hefted the weapon, blue energy and an electric hum coalescing around the blade. In one quick stroke, the ax sheered through the thick PermaSteel door as if it were paper.

Rook smiled at the Warden as Strega carved a hole through the door with ease.

As soon as the two salvagers disappeared into the storage bay, the Warden knelt beside the mumbling man at his feet. "Hey, you're okay. No one's going to hurt you. I promise."

The man's terrified eyes wouldn't make contact, flitting from relived nightmare to imagined terror as his mouth slurred the same words over and over again. "… Hell…

ghosts… dead in the walls… Take me to hell…"

Ramirez knelt at the man's other side. She produced a hypo-syringe from her belt's first-aid kit. "This'll calm him down. Make him a bit more manageable."

The Warden watched as she gently shushed the poor man, calming him with her voice before carefully administering the injection. Ramirez was a strikingly attractive woman with smooth, olive skin, long dark curls, and darker eyes. And she obviously possessed a level of compassionate humanity not shared by the rest of her crew. He found himself wondering how such a woman might become involved with Rook's ragtag band of scavengers.

"One of these things is not like the other."

"What?" Ramirez frowned as they helped the now docile man to his feet.

"Nothing. Come on, let's see if we can find sickbay before your boss lets his pet lizard off its chain."

"I wouldn't joke about that if I were you. Strega is a killer…"

The way she trailed off, the Warden understood the implication. So was Rook.

"Quantum," he said into his com, "we've found a survivor one tier down from where we split up. He's in pretty bad shape. Any chance you might know where we are in relation to the station's med bay?"

"From the readouts I accessed in the control room, I believe you are two tiers above and on the opposite side of medical."

A chorus of howling moans rose from the lower decks, reminding the Warden of something he had read a long, long time ago. Dante's *Inferno*.

He smiled against the hollow feeling in his gut. "Thanks. If you heard that, you know our man isn't responsible for the spooky noises. At least not all of them."

Quantum's voice carried no emotion over the com. "Be careful."

"Sssalvage?" Strega hissed. He and Rook stepped into a supply locker filled with racks of various tools, parts, electronics, and mechanical components.

"No." Rook gave the big room a cursory glance as the automated overhead lights flickered to life. "What we've come for is worth all this junk, the entire station, both ships, and much more besides. Somewhere on this station, my friend, is an experimental Tuatha superdimensional engine. To the right buyer, it'll set us and all our descendants up for life."

The big reptilian's hiss almost sounded like a purr as his green scales took on a bluish hue. "Ssstrega have many off-ssspring. Many des-ssscendantsss."

Rook smiled. "Good. Because when we find that engine, I'm pretty sure the Star Warden and his blue friend aren't going to just let us walk out of here with it. I'm counting on you to make sure that doesn't become a problem."

Strega bared the double row of razored fangs filling his mouth. It could have been a smile, Rook decided. The scariest one he'd seen this side of a childhood nightmare.

"Ssstrega sssolve problem."

The medical bay lit up as soon as the Warden and Ramirez carried the dazed man through the automated door. A med-bot activated as well, its multiple limbs rising from its side, its anthropomorphic head wearing a digital smile.

"How are we doing today? Got a case of the blues, or is it something a little more serious?"

The Warden cringed at the automated doctor as they settled the man onto the first bed. Robotics had taken a decidedly weird branch of evolution since his time. In his day, robots had been robots and people had been people. The medical bot bridged the gap in an unsettling way, at least as far as he was concerned. "Um, he's suffering from some form of mania, possibly post-traumatic in nature. Exhibiting violent behavior and incoherent speech."

"He's been sedated," Ramirez added. "Somunal 7. Two grams."

The robot took this information in with a metallic hum. Its digitized face made the appropriate thoughtful expression as its six arms went to work scanning the new patient. "I see. Abel Carter, Technician First Class. From Mobile Station in the Pleiades. History of hypoglycemia and hypertension. Looks like you've had quite a bad time of it, my friend…"

The Warden motioned Ramirez away from the robot as it continued to administer its automated bedside manner. "We need to see if there are records here that might indicate what happened on this station. You know how to hack a modern computer?"

She wrinkled her nose and grinned. "Hack? What are you, my grandpa? Nobody talks like that anymore. But yeah, I know how to *slide* a 'modern computer.'" She gave him a wink as she walked over to the med bay's terminal. "When we figure out what's going on here, you'll have to share some more of your old-fashioned lingo."

The Warden smiled, his cheeks growing warm. That wink made him feel like a kid again. "It's a date."

The robot's head turned like a mechanical owl, the cartoon face showing a frown and arched eyebrow. "I'm sorry, but that system is restricted to medical personnel only. Please step away from the terminal or I will be forced to engage my security protocols."

"So much for the Hippocratic Oath…" The Warden noted the six elongated appendages, each ending in an array of medical tools that, in a pinch, might be used as weapons. Remembering how his jurisdictional code had bypassed the station's defense systems, he decided to give it another shot. "I am a Star Warden, investigating a possible crime on these premises in pursuant to Star Law 3.42.1. As such, I require access to all systems."

The medical robot clicked and hummed for a moment, the digital face squinting in thought. "I'm sorry, Star Warden, this system does not recognize the authority of Star Law. Please step away from the terminal or I will be forced to kill you both."

The Warden drew and blasted the medical droid to smithereens.

As the smoking robot crumpled to the floor, Ramirez rolled her eyes. "Is that how you deal with everyone who stands up to you?"

The Warden holstered his Comet and turned to her. "Not usually, but I'm a little on edge. And I never did cotton much to robots. Especially those that don't recognize the authority of Star Law… Now, see what you can find on that computer while I tend to our friend, Mr. Carter, here."

Another chorus of disembodied howls sounded through the station's intercoms. A horrific shriek answered from the corridor outside a few moments later.

"Warden," Quantum's voice sounded from his wrist chrono. "Are you there?"

"Yes, what's up?"

"The engineer and her men. They locked me in the upper observatory. I think they mean to head down to the radiation labs."

"Are you okay? Did they attack you?" The Warden glared at Ramirez. She raised her eyebrows in response, shaking her head as if pleading ignorance.

"I am fine. They sealed the door, but I unlocked it quite easily. Should I follow them, or continue searching for the administrator's office?"

"No. Keep 1—"

A horrific shriek came through the open coms channel.

Ramirez's eyes went wide. "That was Hicks."

The coms filled with incoherent babble as half of Rook's crew tried to talk over one another. After a moment of auditory chaos, he bellowed, "Shut the hell up!"

When the coms went silent, Rook said in a more reasonable tone, "Brock, what happened? What's going on?"

She sounded scared, or at least nervous. "I—I'm not sure, Captain. Me, Hicks, and Chan were headed to the lowest tier... we decided to take the lift... The three of us boarded. Then the lights flickered... Hicks screamed... And then he was just gone. Right out of the moving car! Vanished from right beside me..."

Rook chewed on this. "Was the alien with you?"

"No."

"All right. You and Chan stay where you are. Me and Strega are on our way." He flipped on the crew-tracker of his wrist chrono, then motioned the saurian alien to follow him. As they headed down the central winding corridor, he sent a private text to Ramirez:

"*No time to play nice anymore. When you see your shot, take it.*"

Leaving the sedated crewman restrained to his recovery bed, the Warden and Ramirez made their way to the lowest tier. The Warden hoped to head off the rest of Rook's crew. As attractive as he found her to be, he didn't fully trust Ramirez. But as long as he had her at his side, she wasn't at his back.

"You get anything out of that computer?" he asked as they hurried down the spiraling corridor.

Ramirez nodded, pulling up the display on her wrist chrono. "Feeding it to me as we speak. Looks like a wave of nausea and headaches swept through the entire crew about a week ago. Two days later, over a dozen crewmembers came in complaining of bad dreams, and a few admitted to having waking hallucinations… The medical officer prescribed antidepressants and recommended bed rest or lighter duty… These recommendations were denied by the station's administrative officer, citing…"

She looked at the Warden in surprise. "Citing missing crewmembers. The last entry in the medical log was two days ago. The medical officer admits to suffering hallucinations and requests an immediate transfer."

The Warden absorbed this as they reached the lower labs. "What were they fooling around with on this station?"

They entered a prep room where bright yellow hazmat suits hung from the walls and a row of lockers divided the center of the chamber. The heavily sealed door on the opposite side of the room was marked with biohazard and atomic radiation warnings, as well as large-print reminders to double and triple check all safety protocols before entering.

A horrific wail erupted from the left wall. One of the hanging suits moved, fell to the floor. Ramirez gasped, raising her weapon.

A pale, fluttering figure stepped from the wall. It staggered, fell through the row of lockers as if they weren't there. It sprawled on the floor, moaning in agony. Then it sank through the deck as if in water.

Ramirez covered her mouth, her dark eyes wide. "That was Hicks... That was his ghost!"

The Warden stared at the empty floor. "There's no such thing as ghosts."

Brock and Chan were sharing a nic-stick with shaky fingers when Rook and Strega found them sitting at a table in the empty cafeteria. Aside from a few un-bussed tables and an overturned chair, the place looked like any other eatery just before opening. Chrome gleamed, soft music played from the wall speakers, and potted plants stirred in the subtle breeze of air conditioning.

"Any sign of Hicks?" Rook asked, approaching the table.

Brock shook her head, her blue eyes remained downcast. "No... but we saw some... someone or something else..."

"It was a ghost," Chan said before finishing off the smokeless cigarette. "It had to be a ghost. Ran right past us, screaming before vanishing into the bulkhead."

Rook frowned. He checked the environmental readout on his wrist chrono. According to the display, everything was normal. "Maybe there's a chemical leak on that lift or something. Maybe you guys are hallucinating."

Strega licked the air above the two seated crewmembers. "No chemicalsss... Sssomething elssse."

"What?" Brock demanded, finally rising from the table. "What is it, Strega? What do you sense?"

Before the big alien could answer, a chorus of disembodied howls and shrieks echoed from somewhere outside the cafeteria. The lights flickered.

Chan snapped another nic-stick and popped one end in his mouth, his hands still shaking. "Forget this haul, man. We need to get off this hulk before we wind up like Hicks. Ain't no score worth this sh—"

Rook backhanded him out of the chair. "Shut up." Turning to Strega, he said, "What is it? What do you sense on them?"

Ignoring Chan's dazed look as he wiped blood from his lip and got to his feet, Strega said, "Not sssure." He licked the air again. "Tastesss like ssspace, but different." Tilting his big head, he said, "Make sssensssse?"

Rook shook his head. "Hell no, but it's better than another damn ghost story... All right, let's go find the Warden before his blue pal catches up with him. I like the odds of five on one a lot better than five on two."

"What is it?" The Warden whispered into the microphone of the hazmat suit's sealed helmet. He and Ramirez had donned the protective gear and triple checked each other before entering the sealed laboratory. What he saw in the cavernous room's center made him wonder if the suit was protection enough.

"No idea," Ramirez whispered back. "But it's beautiful."

The insulated chamber was bare save for an array of control panels and humming machinery surrounding a shiny, metallic, four-meter-tall ring in the center of the room. Looking into it, the center opened onto a pulsing, shifting vista of multihued energy that whirled and changed like the inside of a kaleidoscope before fixing for a brief moment to display a distant star system... then a storm-wracked beach on some protean world... the icy surface of a hurtling comet... a busy space station orbiting a yellow planet... the infinite pink sky of a gas giant... an epic battle fought near the ragged fringe of a collapsing black hole...

The Warden froze.

He recognized this last image just as it faded into the swirl of hypnotic lights. These then coalesced to reveal a savannah covered in lush blue grass, roamed by a herd of tall, violet-furred and six-legged animals. In that previous brief moment of blaster fire and burning spacecraft, the Warden had seen silvery sleek Ranger-class ships darting among the black and bulbous interdimensional battle cruisers of the Mechtechan.

He had seen the climactic battle of the Continuum War that had ripped him from his own era, his own place in the universe.

"Warden?" Ramirez's tinny mechanical voice came through his suit's speaker. "Are you all right?"

"I'm fine." He didn't tell her he had just found a way back home. Or so he hoped.

"This is clearly what's causing *and* absorbing all the energy output as well as all the mechanical disturbances." Ramirez had a handheld scanner moving among the machinery. She looked up with a frown. "And that cycle is growing stronger by the minute. We need to get out of here."

They hurried from the lab and into the GlasSteel decontamination chamber. As the decon sequence ended, the Warden cast one last, hopeful glance over his shoulder at the strange gate. The gate that might put him and Quantum back in the right place in time.

That glance was why he didn't see Strega's fist when he stepped back into the prep room.

"Keep the suit on." Rook covered the Warden with his blaster pistol as the "great man" removed the hazmat helmet. The Warden sat on the prep room floor where Strega's sucker punch had dropped him. "Nice of you to pull it on over your gun belt. Makes it awful hard to draw, no matter how fast you are."

"What are you doing, Rook?" Ramirez asked in a low voice. "We can't do this... He's a legend out here."

Rook laughed. "Easier and better to kill a legend than a man. At least that's what all the new VR shows say, anyhow."

"I'm no legend." The Warden smiled, rubbing blood from his square chin with the back of his glove. "But if you're thinking about killing me, Rook, I advise against it."

Rook laughed harder, raised an eyebrow. "Oh, I'm sure you would. But, as I'm the curious sort, why would that be, exactly?"

The Warden tilted his head toward the sealed door. "Because of the thing in that lab. I'm guessing you think that's Tuatha tech, which part of it might be. But I've seen that kind of thing once before, back when we fought and drove the Mechtechan out of our universe. *They* made whatever's at the root of that thing in there, and if you want to shut it down, you're probably going to need Quantum's help. He's a Mechtechan."

Rook glanced at Ramirez, who frowned and refused to meet his eye. "And he's not likely to offer that help if I put a hole in you, is that right?"

When the Warden gave a tight smile in reply, Rook asked his first mate, "That what you saw in there?"

Ramirez finally looked at him. "I don't know what I saw. But whatever it is, it's cycling energy at an alarming rate. If you hope to salvage it before it turns this entire system into a blank spot on the charts, then I reckon you'll need the alien's help." She sneered at Brock. "*She* sure won't be able to handle it."

Brock, all but listless until that moment, shot the first mate a murderous look. "Slag you, Ramirez! So long as it runs on juice of one kind or another, I can handle anything!"

"You certainly know how to manipulate a magnetic lock in a hurry."

Rook turned to the prep room's entrance to see the Warden's blue-skinned friend standing in the doorway, his particle rifle at waist level, covering the lot of them.

Frowning at the alien and more at Chan, who should have been watching their back, Rook said, "Easy there... Quantum, was it? No need to get uncivil."

"Uncivil is the last thing I am, sir. And yet my friend shows signs of minor damage." The alien raised the muzzle of his weapon slightly. "How is that civil?"

The Warden started to rise. "I'm fine—"

Strega hissed, brandishing his vibro-ax as the bony protrusions on his skull rose.

The blue alien made a *tsk*ing noise. "No, no, no. I would not do that, my reptilian friend. You are quite large, yes, but your atoms react just like everything else in this universe to a stream of supercharged particles."

"Easy, Strega." Rook sighed and holstered his blaster. If his prize required the help of the Warden's Mechtechan friend to extract, he would just have to resort to diplomacy. As much as he'd like to take the two of them apart and space the remains, he was not foolish enough to risk getting killed, or even wounded, when he was just one room away from the score of a lifetime. "It's okay. We're all friends again."

The Warden got to his feet and started removing the hazmat suit. "I'd not go that far, Captain. But at least we don't have to kill each other."

The part of the man's face not concealed by the black visor told Rook that the unspoken end of that sentence was, *At least not yet.*

The group reconvened in the cafeteria. They sat or stood or leaned in a circle facing each other. No one's back was to anyone else. The Warden stood with his arms folded across his chest, watching Rook and his saurian muscle watch him. Quantum went over the data Ramirez had collected on the hand scanner.

For her part, the salvage ship's first mate looked utterly dejected, sitting with her elbows on her knees, hands folded and head drooped. Ramirez gave the impression of a good person who knew she'd made a bad decision but couldn't find a way out of it. At least the Warden found himself hoping that was the case, along with hoping that he could help her find her path when the current crisis was over and done.

He also found himself hoping that path coincided with his own.

Rook's engineer and her assistant kept throwing nervous glances over their shoulders. Especially when another terrible shriek or unearthly moan would sound from somewhere in the station and the lights would flicker.

"Well?" Rook cleared his throat. "What do you think?"

Quantum's antennae turned slowly, his big, unblinking black eyes still fixed on the scanner. "I think, Captain, that what is in that laboratory is not only responsible for the current laudable state of this facility, but it is also a doomsday weapon in the making."

The Warden cast his partner a glance. "You get that from the data there?"

"Partially. While the rest of you were chasing *ghosts* and double-crossing each other, I located the administrator's office and accessed the station's logs. With that information and the data here, I have deduced a plausible reconstruction of what occurred on this station, as well as a prediction for what is likely to happen next."

Ramirez sat up straight. "Care to share, Quantum? Are we going to die, or what?"

"Not if we leave immediately. But if left unchecked, that device will certainly destroy this system… and possibly more besides."

"What is it, exactly?" Brock asked. "I thought it was just a Tuatha super-dimensional engine, designed to bend the laws of physics in a localized area for experimentation and matter manipulation."

Quantum shook his head. "That is too much of an oversimplification. The device began as an interdimensional reconnaissance probe designed by my people's scientists several millennia ago, as you reckon time. It was obviously assigned to this reality to send back information but was discovered by the civilization you refer to as the Tuatha. The Tuatha, in turn, must have modified the probe's inner workings, allowing them to use the interdimensional data streams to open windows into the space-time continuum.

"And now, the U.P.C. seeks to turn those windows into doorways. Unfortunately, one of this station's crewmembers must have passed through the gate before the technology could be perfected. When his body entered the interdimensional data stream, he was caught in a space-time slip, creating a… a sort of phasal anomaly or time shadow of his former self, which now exists insubstantially in several different times and places simultaneously.

"Furthermore, it would seem this condition is somehow transferrable to other biological entities. So, this unfortunate crewman must have then transmitted this phasal anomaly to others, who in turn have done likewise until the station has become effectively abandoned, save for Mr. Carter now in sickbay."

"The ghosts," Brock said. "That's what happened to Hicks. One of those things turned Hicks into a ghost."

"Phasal anomaly," Quantum corrected. "There are no such things as ghosts."

"A rose by any other name…" Ramirez shook her head.

Quantum shrugged. "The bigger problem at hand is the device. Left open and untended, the gate has since exceeded the regulating capacity of the station's experimental and imperfect framework. I believe the common expression used in such a situation is, *running in the red...*"

"Before we shut it down, we need to consider the crew." The Warden wanted to use the gate to get back to his own place in time, but that selfish notion was low on his list of priorities now. "Is there any way to use it to bring them back? To normal, I mean."

Quantum looked at the data once more. "Sadly, I think not. However, if we close the gate and sever this reality's connection to the space-time continuum, it may return them to their original physical states. Though there is no way to predict which part of the multiverse in which that original state will find itself. Nor what permanent effect their sojourn in the space-time slip will have had on their individual psyches. Judging by the sounds we have heard, I can only assume that most of them are quite irrevocably insane at this point."

The Warden shook his head in frustration.

Rook rubbed the stubble on his chin. "Then how do we close it?"

The lights went out.

The whole station shuddered.

Artificial gravity failed. The Warden lost contact with the floor.

A spectral scream ripped through the darkened room.

The Warden tapped his visor, turning the gloom to emerald light.

A trio of glowing wraiths emerged from the wall behind Chan and Brock. The haggard, maddened specters moved in quick, jerky steps, claw-like hands outstretched, hollow eyes and distended mouths filled with pale white fire.

"Look out!" The Warden drew his blasters and fired on the three phasal anomalies.

The glowing bolts went through them as if they were nothing more than holograms. The ghostly crewmen reached Chan. One of the errant blaster bolts struck the food printer behind him. It exploded in a shower of sparks and arcs of electricity.

The lights came up, and gravity was restored. The Warden shut his eyes at the blinding effect on his visor as he toppled to the floor. With a grunt he switched back to normal vision.

"What the hell was that?" Rook growled as he tried to regain his feet.

"Chan! He's gone!" Brock shouted. She cast a hateful glance at the Warden. "Look! He's got his guns out. He tried to kill me and Chan!"

"No." Strega said. The big saurian hadn't been upended by the sudden change in gravity, owing to his thick toe talons digging into the carpeted floor. "Warden fired on ghostsss."

"Phasal anomalies," Quantum said, returning to his feet. "I saw them, too. They were somehow… banished by the explosion of the appliance, though that may have been a coincidence."

"You know what Einstein said about coincidences," Ramirez said as she stepped to the smoking food printers. "These are older models, they run on direct current. You think that might have something to do with your 'phasal anomalies'?"

"More importantly," Rook said, looking at his wrist chrono. "That blackout was caused by a massive spike in energy. And that spike is still climbing."

The Warden headed for the door. "We need to get back to the lab."

As the others followed the Warden from the cafeteria, Rook grabbed Brock by the arm. "I want you to go to sickbay," he whispered in her ear. "Space the nut-job recuperating up there. With no surviving crew, the Star Warden and his blue pal have no reason to stand in the way of our salvage. Even if this… *whatever* it is down there turns out to be too hot to handle, everything on this station is ours."

Narrowing her blue eyes, Brock gave one curt nod and set off back up the spiraling corridor to the right. Rook turned left and went after the others.

Rounding the curved wall outside the lab's prep room, he saw a violent purple and crimson glow washing over the entire corridor. The strange illumination came from the prep room's opened door. When Rook looked in to see the source, he sagged against the doorframe, mouth slack and eyes wide.

The Warden, his Mechtechan friend, Strega, and Ramirez stood just inside the room, apparently just as stunned. The other side of the chamber was gone, just an opened hole into space. The ragged edges of that hole writhed and glimmered with the violet and garnet light. So fascinating was the spectacle that it took Rook a moment to realize the view of open space shifted from vista to impossible vista.

"What the hell…?"

"Everybody out," the Warden said. "Hurry! We've got to seal this chamber."

When everyone was safely outside the prep room, the Warden activated the door's mag lock. The action gave the illusion of safety, but they had all seen the impossible horror on the other side of the thin wall of insulated aluminum and PlaSteel.

For a moment or two, no one spoke.

Rook cleared his throat. "What the hell is that? How come we weren't spaced through that breach?"

The Mechtechan was nonplussed. "Because that is not a breach into space. At least not as you understand it. This station is still intact, more or less."

Ramirez shook her head. She was pale, her jaw tight. "I don't understand."

The Warden answered. "The station is entering the space-time slip, just like the crew… But how, Quantum? I thought you said it only affected biological matter."

The alien's brow arched over his big black left eye, antennae writhing. "The energy cycle. It must have reached a threshold of some kind, whereby the rate of cycle has increased exponentially. There is no way to tell how quickly the slip will grow, but eventually the entire station and all aboard it will be trapped as phasal anomalies in the space-time continuum.

"There is also no way to tell just how big the slip will become. It could continue to grow until it devours this entire system, or possibly more…"

A woman's scream from somewhere above ended the conversation.

"Where's Brock?" the Warden asked Rook.

"Don't know. She was right behind me." He turned and led the group up the spiraling corridor, headed for sickbay.

Unearthly moans surrounded them every step of the way. The time shadows' suffering seemed to increase in proportion to the size of the growing rift. The Warden tried not to imagine the agony those poor people were going through. An agony he was unable to end.

Brock lay sprawled just outside the medical facility. The Warden knelt beside the stunned engineer. A deep cut marred her forehead. But she was alive.

"The crewman... Carter. He's gone." Ramirez swept the empty med bay with her submachinegun. "Looks like Brock released him."

"He's... got my gun," Brock slurred.

The Warden helped the groggy woman to her feet. "Get her in there and check her out. As soon as she can talk, I've got some questions for her... In the meantime, I think you and I should have a chat, Captain."

Rook's wolfish grin returned. "Happy to oblige, Warden."

The Warden motioned him to follow. "And you can leave Strega behind. I'm not going to hurt you."

Rook chuckled as if to say, *I'd like to see you try.*

A dozen meters from the med bay, the Warden halted in the alcove of a darkened lounge area. "Okay, Rook, let's put our cards on the table. We've established you knew about whatever is—or *was* down in that lab, and that's why you're here. Not because of the distress call."

Rook feigned innocence. "You wound me, Warden."

"I'm betting you sent Brock up here to remove Carter from the equation, freeing you up to salvage the entire station. But here's the rub, Captain: if we don't work together and figure out a way to stop what's happening down on the lowest tier, there won't be a station to salvage."

Rook shrugged. "There's still enough untended equipment on the upper tiers to make this a profitable venture, even with the loss of two of my crew, Warden. And if that's the play I decide to make, I don't think you and your blue friend can stop me."

The Warden sighed. Maybe he and Quantum could stop the looters, but at what cost? A shootout on a dying space station that would only result in a few more corpses—an act of "justice" far removed from any inhabited system. Rook was just like the medical robot he'd destroyed. He didn't recognize Star Law. At least not as the Warden did.

"All right. Get your people together and take as much as you can in the next hour. Then get off this station."

Rook's smile faltered. "I thought you wanted our help."

The Warden still clung to the fading hope of repairing the breach and freeing the doomed crew from their tormented existence as "ghosts." And, in the back of his mind lurked the desperate thought of somehow using the gate to get back to his own place in time. That slim, selfish hope hinged on the cooperation of Rook and his people.

"I do. But I can't focus on fixing that hole in space and time while looking over my shoulder for the next sucker punch. Quantum and I will do it on our own."

"It'll take more than an hour to salvage enough to turn a profit. Make it three."

The Warden gave a bitter laugh. "I don't even know if we have the one hour before that interdimensional hole swallows us. But I'll give you one, that's it."

Rook's grin returned. "Suit yourself. Just remember you've got a crackpot with a shotgun running loose on this station as well as all them ghosts your blue boy says don't exist."

"Don't worry about us. Just get your stuff and go." The Warden headed back in the direction of sickbay.

Rook cursed under his breath, then called after him. "All right. Have it your way, Warden. We'll play nice and help you fix that breach if we can. But if I'm going to take that kind of risk, I want full salvage when this is done."

The Warden stopped and frowned. "Only if it's legal. But if I catch you or any member of your crew trying to kill Carter or any other survivors, I won't hesitate to put you down."

A quartet of screaming ghosts shambled out of the lounge's far wall. They lumbered across the room before sinking through the floor. Their shrieks continued to echo throughout the station.

"First things first," the Warden said. "We'll need to find a way to defend ourselves against those."

"You said something about the food processors in the cafeteria," Rook said to Ramirez as he and the Warden returned to sickbay. "Something about them running on direct current."

"Yes. Most stuff nowadays uses alternating current. Safer and more efficient, but that model of food printer uses DC and works faster."

The Warden's alien spoke up. "When the device exploded, it expelled an arc of direct current, which somehow… disrupted the time shadows. It is possible that the constant stream of electrons breaks the phasal anomaly's connection with this plane in the time-space continuum. At least temporarily."

The Warden nodded. "That'll have to be good enough. So, how do we arm ourselves with some direct current?"

Brock, more cognizant with a bandaged forehead, said, "My welder uses direct current. Doesn't have the range of even a hold-out pistol, but it could do in a pinch."

Rook snapped his fingers and turned to Strega. "That supply closet we checked upstairs. It was a repair and maintenance storeroom. If there's gonna be any industrial-strength welders on this hulk, they'll be there."

"Some welders use alternating current," Ramirez pointed out.

"I can alter them to produce direct current," the Mechtechan said.

"Right." The Warden turned for the door. "Then I'll take Rook and Strega to fetch the welders. Quantum, I want you and the ladies to work out a way to shut down that interdimensional hole that's trying to eat us."

The alien's antennae twirled, and he seemed to smile. "Certainly, if you insist on giving me the easy job."

Rook and Strega followed the Warden into the central corridor. They hadn't gone a dozen steps to the right, heading up, when what sounded like a hundred howls filled the hall behind them.

Rook turned to see a host of apparitions erupting from the walls, ceiling and floor. Though vaguely human in shape, the spectral figures were elongated, twisted, and malformed. Shrieking faces melted and distended over warped skulls as spidery fingers and hands stretched out toward him.

For a moment, Rook thought he saw the disfigured shades of Hicks and Chan in that roiling ectoplasmic mass.

He froze.

"Run!" The Warden grabbed his shoulder, roughly pushed him forward.

He ran.

The horde of ghosts followed, slithering, boiling, crawling, and scurrying along every surface of the spiraling corridor, the hellish volume of their insane suffering rising above the blood pounding in Rook's ears, the breath tearing at his throat, the heartbeat drumming in his chest with each frantic step.

"They're not stopping!" Rook gasped.

The Warden turned to Strega. "What's that vibro-ax run on?"

The big saurian shrugged. "Power?"

"Worth a shot." The Warden snatched the hefty weapon off Strega's back, turned, and hurled it into the closing horror. As the vibro-ax tumbled into the first wave, the Warden drew one of his blasters and fired. The shot caught the power supply in the haft, and the weapon exploded in a blinding arc of white electricity.

The ghosts vanished.

Rook looked at the Warden. A single bead of sweat on the man's nose was the only evidence of the harrowing chase. The Warden shrugged and holstered his weapon. "I had a fifty-fifty chance and took it. Now, let's get those welders."

"Yes. Let's."

"Any luck figuring out how to stop this thing?" the Warden asked as he, Rook, and Strega set three heavy welders on an empty bed in the med bay.

Another pulse shook the station, killing the lights and gravity. Ghastly moans sounded outside the sealed doors.

Quantum turned from the computer as the lights and artificial-G came back online. "As a matter of fact, yes. I have a plan that may work. By running high-capacity conduits from the power plant directly into the rift, we may be able to channel all the station's energy into enough direct current to disrupt the opened channel. If I am right, this disruption may give someone enough time to reach the gate's controls and shut it down manually."

Rook scoffed. "*If* you're right. That's one hell of a big if."

Quantum looked at the salvage captain. "If I am wrong, we will all die unless we leave this station and system immediately."

The Warden trusted his friend's judgment, especially when it came to matters of science and technology. More than enough to bet his life on it.

But Rook grunted, looked to Ramirez and Brock. "What do you guys think?"

Brock shrugged. "Sounds as good as any solution to me. But my vote is to loot and scoot. This is some serious cosmic mojo we're slagging with, Rook."

The Warden watched Ramirez. She raised her chin and looked Rook in the eye. "We came to plunder this place, but we might just be able to save it. And by doing so, we might get Hicks and Chan back. I think that's worth the risk."

The Warden nodded. "Well said. Let's get to work."

Rook shook his head, but said nothing.

Ten minutes later, Quantum monitored the situation from the med bay while the Warden led the others back to the supply closets to retrieve several hundred meters of high-voltage cable. They had converted the industrial welders to direct current, and Quantum had connected the medical terminal to all the station's higher functions.

The welders, designed for repairing the hulls of spacecraft, were bulky affairs that necessitated the use of both hands and a heavy charging pack. While not typically a major issue in the low gravity of space, this required one person to carry the welder and another to carry the pack while in the station's artificial gravity. Brock and Ramirez carried the welders, and Rook and the Warden wore their packs, respectively. Only Strega was strong enough to simultaneously do both.

The plan entailed retrieving the cables, then making straight for the central power plant where Brock would hook them into the primary generator. She would then change the output settings to direct current. From there, they would make their way to the lowest level and deposit the other ends of the cables into the maw of the rift. When all was ready, Quantum would engage the generator from his station at the computer.

That was the plan. But the Warden knew that no plan survives first contact with the enemy intact.

"I'm curious," he said to Ramirez as they led the way to the engine room. He and Rook now carried a heavy spool of cable in each hand, as well as the power packs on their backs. The welder teams were spaced several meters apart to keep from being completely wiped out by a sudden rush of ghosts from the walls or ceiling. "How did you wind up with this outfit?"

Ramirez smiled sidelong at him. She now wore dark goggles to protect against the welder's glare. "You mean, 'What's a nice girl like you doing in a place like this?' Isn't that a pickup line from your generation?"

The Warden laughed for what felt like the first time in forever. "Actually, that one was pretty old before I was born, I do believe. But yes, essentially, that's what I'm asking."

A wailing head poked out of the floor in front of them. Ramirez blasted it with a white rope of direct current. A smoking scorch mark on the melted rubberized floor remained.

They continued down the corridor.

"So, we're sharing our life stories now?" Her smile returned with a sigh. "I've made a lot of bad decisions, Warden, and I don't think right now is the best time to catalog them for somebody whose name I don't even know."

The Warden glanced over his shoulder, saw that Rook and Brock were well out of earshot. "My name is—"

A gunshot drowned out his whispered words.

The wind rushed from his lungs as his knees gave out. The impact knocked him sideways into the wall.

It took the Warden a moment to realize he'd been shot.

In that moment Ramirez raised the welder and sent an arc of electricity down the hallway. By its blue-white glow, the Warden saw the shaggy head of Carter duck around the next bend.

"No!" the Warden shouted, regaining his breath as he tried to stand. "Don't kill him!"

"What the hell's going on?" Rook demanded as he and Brock hurried to his side. "That was no ghost."

"It was Carter." Ramirez scowled at the engineer. "With Brock's shotgun."

"Did you get him?" Rook asked, hope evident in his tone.

The Warden finally managed to regain his feet. He checked his bleeding side. The shock was wearing off, fiery pins and needles rapidly replacing the numb sensation. "No, she didn't. The man's out of his mind, not responsible for his actions."

Ramirez stared at him. "He just shot you!"

The Warden shook his head. "My suit took most of the trauma. Just a flesh wound. Glad it was buckshot and not an AP slug... Come on, we've got a job to do and we can't be bunched up like this."

"Right," Rook said. "Hate for that psycho to get more than one of us with that scattergun. But you stand on your moral high ground, Warden. And just maybe the next blast *won't* catch you in that pretty face of yours."

The lights flickered, went out with the gravity. Moans and shrieks sounded from all sides. The lights did not come back on. The howls grew louder, closer.

"Form a circle," the Warden said, drifting weightless in the black. Touching his visor, the world turned green. A nightmare world of screeching, disfigured faces and clawing hands.

Shouts, curses, and screams from beside him joined the harrowing cacophony.

He grabbed his floating companions, turned them to face outward. To face the nightmare surrounding, enveloping them. "Fire!"

Three blinding jets of electricity seared the thinning air, filling his nostrils with burnt ozone and his eyes with white blindness. The sizzle and crackle of direct current continued for several moments.

The screams ended.

He crashed to the floor amid a chaos of limbs and torsos.

"Light's back on!" Rook grunted. "Get up and get offa me."

The Warden switched his visor back to normal vision. The specters were gone.

And so was Ramirez.

Rook watched the Warden's back as he led them deeper into the accursed station. He could sense the rage boiling off the mysterious lawman. Straining against the weight of the heavy spools in his hands, the Warden moved with a violent purpose. He'd allowed them to patch up his side, but he'd refused to go back to medical in spite of the blood loss and tissue trauma.

Which, all things considered, was perfectly fine by Rook.

He didn't mind letting the Warden take point. Let the uppity bastard be the next one snatched by the ghosties or become target practice for the whacko with the shotgun. That'd just leave the blue beanpole alien to deal with when the dust settled. What bothered Rook was the notion that the Warden hadn't seemed truly angry until Ramirez vanished.

And that anger suddenly inspired the barest inkling of fear in Rook's gut.

Rook wasn't used to fear. To his way of thinking, it was a useless sensation. Something that either made you freeze up in the face of danger, flee from opportunities, or take stupid risks. Despite all the crazy, weird nonsense he'd seen since boarding this station, Rook hadn't known a moment of fear. Not until now.

He'd already decided he hated the Warden. But now, he realized, he feared him.

And Rook just couldn't abide being afraid of any man.

"What to do about it?"

"What?" Brock asked beside him.

Rook glanced at her. "Just thinking out loud… It occurs to me that if this alien's plan works, we might save the station, but we could be trapped on it with a boatload of nut-jobs crazier than the one toting your weapon… Just something to chew on."

"It wasn't supposed to be like this…"

Rook raised an eyebrow. "What did you say?"

Brock shook her head. "Nothing. I'm just scared… Look, we're almost to the power plant."

The automated doors opened, and the lights came up. The Warden led the remaining salvagers into the power plant, a towering circular chamber built around the atomic heart of the facility. The reactor was probably no larger than a good-sized lavatory, but the protective casing surrounding it looked like a glistening metallic cylinder ten meters wide and fifteen tall. Most of this surface area glimmered and flashed with readout displays and control panels, or it bristled with reinforced PermaSteel couplings feeding into energy conduits.

The nuclear behemoth was far and away outside the Warden's level of technological acumen. He turned to Brock, trying hard not to blame her for freeing and arming Carter. If the madman hadn't ambushed them, they might not have been swarmed by the phasal anomalies. Ramirez might still be with them. He might have a reason to stay in this time.

"Well, let's get started."

Brock glared at him. "Just watch my back. If I get ghosted before these settings are reconfigured, you lot won't be far behind me."

Rook dropped his spools of cable at Brock's feet. "Just shut up and get to work." Taking her welder, he slid out of the power pack. "Strega, you watch the door. Me and the Warden will go up to that catwalk and walk the perimeter."

The Warden picked up the pack and followed Rook as he climbed the metal steps. "I take it you want to talk."

Rook glanced at him. "You could say that… I don't know what happened between you and Ramirez in that med bay—"

The Warden grabbed him, almost spinning the bigger man off the stair. "Nothing happened." He spoke through gnashed teeth. "And I don't like the insinuation."

Rook snarled, freeing himself from the Warden's grip. "Fine. Like I said, I don't know, and I don't care. I just want to make sure you don't hold me responsible for what happened to her. She was a member of *my* crew, after all."

The Warden took a deep breath. "Right. I can see how their loss has taken its toll on you. You're all broke up."

Rook's wicked grin returned. "Salvage is a tough job, Warden. It pays, but it don't pay enough to get attached. I thought someone like you'd understand that, seeing as how you're the last of *your* crew."

The Warden narrowed his eyes behind his visor. Staring at that wolfish grin, he knew he'd made a mistake by letting Rook and his people stay on the station. He'd let his foolish hope of getting back to his own time cloud his judgment. That had fooled him into thinking there had been a connection with Ramirez, which had only lowered his guard even more. The imagined connection had ultimately gotten her killed.

He had no right to blame Rook or Brock, or even Carter, or anyone else for that matter. It was his fault.

"Got it," the engineer called from below. "Now, let's get the other ends of these cables down and into that hole."

Rook carried the two spools again, carefully feeding the high-voltage cables behind him. Again, he let the Warden lead the way to the lower decks, carrying his own pair of spools. The going was much slower now, and they only had Strega's welder for security. Carrying a supply pack tethered to another person while feeding the cables was just too unwieldy a process. Brock carried her pistol in one hand, her small welder in the other, keeping an eye out for Carter's next ambush or the next ghost attack.

The lights continued to flicker, and each step made Rook feel drunk. The gravity wasn't constant, fluctuating between low-G and heavy-G with each pulse of the overhead fluorescents. The walls and decks creaked, rattled and groaned, sometimes louder than the constant wail and moan of the unseen wraiths.

"That's new." Rook glanced at Brock. "Think it's what you did in the power plant?"

Brock shrugged, gave him a blank look.

"Quantum." The Warden tapped his com. "What's happening to the structural integrity?"

The alien's voice came over the open channel. "The rift is widening. It appears that some incarnations of the station within the trans-dimensional void are breaking up. This is having a rippling effect across the space-time continuum."

Rook growled. "In modern cant, if you don't mind."

"The big hole you saw earlier that I told you was not actually a hole in the station? Well, now it is a hole. At least in some realities, and it is spreading across all realities like a shockwave across water."

Rook grunted. "Then we'd best hurry."

The Warden had already broken into a dead run, the spools in his hands making a sizzling, whirring sound as the thick black cables unfurled behind him.

Rook shook his head. "Ain't no way we can keep up with you, Warden! Slow down!"

The Warden didn't answer as he disappeared around the next curve. A splash of brilliant red and violet light painted the walls at that curve. Gravity came back at full strength.

But on the wrong axis.

Rook and his remaining crew plummeted straight for the glowing wall as if they'd fallen through a trap door.

The Warden stepped from the corridor and into infinity.

One second, he ran through the station's flickering lights and curving halls, the next he fell into the cosmic void of the space-time continuum. He let go of one spool and grabbed the cable of the other.

After a moment or a century, he stopped falling.

Hanging from the cable, he stared at the vast array of ultimate mysteries unfolding around him. In the blink of an eye, stars were born, lived millions of years, and died in apocalyptic conflagrations or simply faded to nothing. Species rose from primordial muck to found vast, interstellar empires before descending back into elemental chaos. Perspective and time were meaningless in the void. The Warden hung a hand's breath from the surface of a flaring sun within a Dyson sphere one instant, then hovered above a crowd of barbaric humanoids on the hunt the next.

The experience was at once soul-rending, mind-shattering, and... exquisitely beautiful.

As the vista shifted and coalesced, the Warden noticed something familiar. An armada of hulking alien ships battled a swarm of sleek silver craft at the edge of a black hole. Straining his eyes, he watched as the *Ranger VII* landed on the alien flagship alongside three other Star Warden ships.

He and seven other Wardens boarded the enemy command ship with the intent to force it into the black hole's event horizon.

"If I could only reach them... reach me..."

The Warden stretched out his right hand, willing the perspective to change as it had so many times during the eons he hung suspended in the void.

"Warden!"

A huge figure dropped into his vision. Followed by two more people. These also clung to the high-voltage cables.

It took the Warden several moments or decades to recognize Rook, Brock, and Strega. Their bodies shifted and warped, fractaling across every racial and gender spectrum, as if an infinity of possibilities were being shuffled to determine the exact circumstances that might define these individuals. Gradually they coalesced into the familiar forms they had worn on the station in their native reality.

"What the hell?" Rook gasped, sweat glistening on his stubbled, wide-eyed face.

Brock shut her eyes tight and vomited.

Strega clung to the cable, breathing heavily, the bone ridges on his head flaring up and down like a bellows.

The vision of the battle at the edge of the black hole vanished, replaced by the sight of pieces of flaming debris descending on a barren world in a tiny system shrouded in the cloud of an ancient comet.

The Warden closed his extended fist and shook his head. "We've got to climb back up and into what's left of the station so Quantum can flip the switch."

Rook looked up the cable. "Then let's go."

The ascent was maddening. They could see the lip of the rift above, like a jagged window onto the station. But it was never constant. One moment it was within arm's reach, the next it seemed a kilometer away. At times, they climbed for unknown hours without seeing the opening move at all.

And then, without warning, the Warden hauled himself back onto the rubberized deck of the station. He turned and helped Rook and the others over the lip of the rift. The four of them knelt or lay on the deck, panting and solemn.

"Warden?" Quantum's voice came over the coms. "Are you there, Warden? What's going on?"

Regaining his feet, the Warden took a deep breath to respond. In that instant, he caught a nod from Rook. His instincts warned him a split second before Strega moved.

The huge saurian struck with preternatural speed. Forewarned, the Warden rolled with the impact. He used his judo training to flip Strega across his body. The alien had hoped to bull-rush him into the opened rift.

Instead, Strega was the one who had fallen.

The Warden found himself again stretched out on the deck. This time he held Strega's massive wrist with both hands to keep the reptilian bruiser from tumbling into infinity.

He heard Rook step behind him. Heard the man's blaster pistol clear its plastic holster. Straining against the burning pain in his arms and shoulders, the Warden said through gnashed teeth, "Rook, you shoot me and Strega dies."

He was not surprised by the reply. "With what I'll make off this station, it won't be hard to hire a whole new crew, Warden... I wish I could say it's nothing personal, that it's just business. But, truth to tell, I never liked you from the moment I set eyes on you. And you know what? I thought you'd be taller."

"Rook." It was Brock's voice. "You don't need to do this. We can still make out okay with what's not battened down on the station once we close this rift. Nobody else needs to die."

"Shut up." Rook's voice was cruel and gloating, savoring the moment. "Just be ready. Once this thing closes, the first thing we're lifting is whatever is in that lab."

The Warden's grip weakened. Fire raged up and down the muscles of his upper body. He looked into Strega's emotionless eyes. "Hold on. Just don't let go." Though he knew they were both about to die.

A gunshot boomed behind him.

The Warden winced, expecting oblivion. But it wasn't a blaster shot. It was a ballistic firearm.

Screams and shouts... more shots... blaster fire...

Someone stepped on the Warden's back, tripped, and fell over his head.

He looked up to see two figures tumble into the star-filled rift. A terrified Rook struggled against a bloody and gibbering Carter. Locked in a mortal embrace, they struck Strega's broad back and bounced. The impact knocked the massive alien from the Warden's failing grasp. All three disappeared into the shimmering infinity of the space-time continuum.

The Warden stared a moment longer, waiting for the image of the battle at the black hole to return.

"Warden." Brock grabbed his shoulder. "Come on. We've got to go."

He shook off the growing ennui and rose to his feet. With a nod, he followed her up the corridor at a run. "Quantum, we're clear. Flip the switch."

"Affirmative."

A pulse of energy surged through the station, hummed through the high-voltage cables at their feet. The stale air smelled of burning ozone, and the overhead lighting flickered and went out. The walls and bulkheads creaked, shuddered, and groaned. The sound of a titanic explosion reverberated from the lowest decks.

The shockwave hit a moment later.

Knocked to the floor, the Warden gasped for breath and tried to stand. The deck shook and swayed as gravity shifted on multiple axes. A wave of nausea hit him with the force of one of Strega's punches. The Warden staggered, helped Brock to her feet, and kept moving.

"Quantum! What's happening?"

"I... I believe it is working."

"You couldn't tell by me."

The lights came up and gravity settled back to normal. The Warden and Brock stumbled against the automated doors and fell into the medical bay.

Rolling over onto his back, the Warden stared at Quantum seated at the computer terminal. "Status report."

Quantum glanced at the console. "All systems normal. Hull integrity at one hundred percent... Security cameras back online, displaying no anomalies. It appears the rift is closed. Apparently, the direct current also shorted out the gate's circuitry. You were successful."

They sat in silence for a while, absorbing this. Brock exhaled and closed her eyes. "Hear that? Quiet... No ghosts."

The Warden pushed his bruised and battered body up against the wall, feeling anything but successful. "What about life signs? The crew?" He thought of Ramirez, hoping she, at least, was somewhere safe and sane on the station.

Quantum shook his head. "I am sorry. We three are the only persons aboard the station at present."

The Warden rubbed his face. "What a nightmare... I am curious about one thing, however." He turned to Brock. "I overheard you say something to Rook on the way to the power plant. You said, 'It wasn't supposed to be like this.'"

Brock dropped her gaze, but not before the Warden saw tears forming. She took another deep breath, rubbed her smudged nose. "I'm with the Frontier Freedom Society."

The Warden and Quantum exchanged blank looks and waited for elaboration.

"You haven't heard of the F.F.S.? We're dedicated to forcing the United Planetary Council to reopen the Frontier to independent colonization, without having to jump through all the corporate slag."

Quantum suggested, "An Undoc militant organization?"

"Something like that. Freedom fighters if your family is starving to death on an overpopulated, overtaxed planet in the Civilized Worlds or eking out subsistence on a barren rock while hiding from government agents somewhere on the Frontier. Terrorists to the corporations and the politicians suckling on their bloated teats."

The Warden hated this new era in which he found himself. Too many gray areas, and not enough lit in clean, clear black and white. He shook his head, wondering if it had ever been that simple, even in his own time. "What's all that got to do with this station?"

Brock cleared her throat. "We had a man here, in deep cover. He was just supposed to do a little sabotage and gain enough intel so we could force the U.P.C. to back off, lest we leak the story to the independent press."

The Warden sighed. "But it all went wrong."

"We knew they had some Tuatha tech and were conducting unlicensed experimentation. We just didn't know how dangerous it was... So, what are you going to do with me now?"

The Warden stared at her, but Brock didn't flinch. She was willing to face the music. And though he knew she had been about to space Carter at Rook's behest, he couldn't forget that she could have shot him while he lay staring into the void. Or even just left him there.

Instead, she had gotten him on his feet and moving.

The Warden stood. "Quantum and I are going down to that lab to disassemble and destroy the gate. If you're still here when we get back, I'll have no choice but to put you in a detention cell until we can get a Star Cav ship out here for processing."

With that he led Quantum out of the med bay, confident she and the *Magpie 6* would be long gone before they were done with their task.

As they reached the now-restored laboratory, the Warden paused to face Quantum. "How was it, do you suppose, that we were able to enter the space-time rift and come back out without becoming time shadows like the crew?"

Quantum shrugged. "I would speculate that as the rift grew stronger, it also grew more stable in this reality. Thus, it would be less destructive to your atomic structure. Of course, without more data, that is only an educated guess. Would you like me to conduct an extensive study into the phenomenon?"

The Warden opened the lab door. "Nope. I'm ready to put this place as far behind me as possible. Let's destroy that gate. After, we'll send an anonymous message to the U.P.C., letting them know their new toy is broken... On our way out the door, of course."

The Warden thought about that brief moment where he was so close to returning to his own time. He had helped to save his reality then, but if he hadn't been hurled into this era by that act, he would not have been able to save it this time.

He thought about Ramirez, a stranger for whom he'd felt something he hadn't felt for anyone in a very long time. That feeling, that attraction, had reminded him that he was still a man of flesh and blood, and not just a mission or a purpose. It also reminded him that he did not have to be alone in this new era.

As tragic as the encounter on this station had been, it had demonstrated that the Warden was, in fact, exactly where he was supposed to be.

CITY OF THE Mad God

The sleek, if obsolete, *Ranger VII* slid effortlessly through the infinite void of Frontier Space, the light from a billion stars shimmering along its silvery hull. After their most recent adventure, the Last Star Warden decided to slow-travel through conventional space for a while so both he and the ship could recuperate.

For his part, Quantum, the Warden's interdimensional companion, seemed unflappable, no matter how harrowing or unnerving an ordeal proved to be.

The Warden lay stretched out on his bunk in the small crew compartment, staring at the metal ceiling, wishing he was as stoic as his blue-skinned friend, as stoic as the Frontier legends claimed him to be. But the truth, like the truth behind all legends, was far less glorious and far more complicated. He was simply a mortal man. He bruised and bled just like every other human being in the galaxy.

And like many among his now lost generation, the Warden had simply been trained to overcome those vulnerabilities, to keep them hidden. Trained in a system that had perished nearly a century ago, a system created by a society that was no more. At least as he had known it.

Even as the Warden had saved his universe from an extra-dimensional invasion, he had been ripped from it and hurled into its future to such an extent that his world no longer existed. Not in any real sense. True, he now traveled among star systems peopled by the descendants of his own contemporaries, but he may as well have occupied the parallel universe from which Quantum's people, the Mechtechan, had launched their failed invasion.

For all that, the Warden remained hopeful. Hopeful that he could find some remnant of the morality and optimism that had characterized his own era in this new, jaded one defined by corruption, greed, and nihilism. But, almost without fail thus far, it seemed that every time he found some small glimmer of that hope reflected back at him, it was summarily snuffed out by whatever fell circumstances the cruel and uncaring Cosmos chose to dish out.

He thought of Ramirez, the woman who had so perfectly embodied this era's dichotomies while inspiring the Warden's personal interest. He shook his head. "I never even learned her first name."

"Warden," Quantum called from the controls. "We are receiving a priority message. It is addressed specifically to you."

The Warden sighed. He hadn't been in this new timeline a standard year, and already half the Frontier needed him, had come to rely upon him for justice. The other half tended to want him dead, and for that same reason. "On my way."

Hovering up the short corridor between the crew compartment and the cockpit, the Warden slid into the pilot's chair. "What have we got?"

Quantum's short antennae whirred slowly above his oversized black eyes. "It is a prerecorded message originating on Cibola Seven, a mining interest in the Praxis Gargantua Nebula. The time stamp indicates it was sent less than six standard hours ago, meaning it has Alpha One priority, given our relative position to the colony's location."

The Warden grunted as the dimly lit image of a disheveled, hollow-eyed man filled the display. He appeared to be middle-aged, with flowing white hair and a droopy moustache, his lined face studded with a silvery beard. A dark uniform of some kind hung loosely from his broad shoulders, the collar open around his thick neck.

"Warden," the man said into the camera, his deep voice raspy and overused. "My name is Maximo Ryan, Chief Constable of Cibola Seven…" He turned sharply to peer at something outside the camera's view, his pale eyes narrowing. "What was that…?" After a pause, the man muttered to himself. "Nothing… Something… Where was I? Oh, yes… Warden, I need your help. There've been… murders. Murders nobody's talking about… the bodies are missing… Not only that…"

Again something off-camera distracted the man. Jumping to his feet, he shouted,

"Who's there? I'm warning you, I'm armed!"

The Warden and Quantum exchanged looks.

After moving around the camera for a bit, Chief Constable Ryan finally returned to conclude his message. "Please, Warden. You've got to come, and come soon... There's something going on here on Cibola Seven..." He licked his lips, face so close to the camera the Warden could see tears filling his bloodshot eyes. "I think... I think it's some kind of conspiracy... I think they're in on it with *him*, and they know I'm onto them... I think he's trying to drive me mad..." He jerked his head away again as if listening.

Shoving his face against the camera, Ryan hissed, "Hurry! There isn't much time!"

When the message ended, the Warden and Quantum stared at the blank screen in silence.

"That was... certainly interesting..." Quantum rubbed his undersized chin.

The Warden ran the message back and paused it on the image of Constable Ryan's wild-eyed face. "Set a course for Cibola Seven."

"You are aware that man shows signs of mental instability and paranoia. This could be a simple case of contacting the local authorities and suggesting they help him get medical assistance."

The Warden closed the display and turned to face Quantum. "True. But he obviously holds a position of authority, and he's probably armed. If he is suffering some sort of psychotic break, he could pose a threat not only to himself but also to others. Besides... there's an old Earth axiom that says, 'Just because you're paranoid, it doesn't mean they're not out to get you.'"

Quantum's huge eyes narrowed, and his childlike mouth flattened. "And who are 'they' in this specific situation?"

"That's what I want to find out."

Cibola Seven occupied a rather large asteroid at the heart of a dense, mineral-rich belt on the fringes of the Praxis Gargantua Nebula. A steady stream of commercial and tourist traffic moved between the colony and the nearest Einstein-Rosen bridge.

"Who owns Cibola Seven?" the Warden asked, watching the line of heavy corporate freighters emerge from the violet and pink gases of the nebula. "I see six different logos on those ships, all big Earth corporations save for that one. Looks like C-7 over a silver skyline. A local company?"

Quantum glanced at a data display. "Cibola Seven is an independent interest, owned by the local population. It was founded by Undoc settlers shortly after the Breakthrough around two standard decades ago. Its sovereignty appears to be unofficially recognized by both the major corporations and the United Planetary Council."

"That's odd. Or at least very unusual. The place has become so successful in that short a time that they can hold their own against the corporations and the U.P.C., in defiance of the non-settlement laws? And they've done it so well they even flaunt it with a thriving tourist industry…"

"Mostly gambling establishments and pleasure resorts," Quantum offered. "The colony supplies 27.9 percent of the galaxy's growing lithium requirements, giving them a considerable advantage when negotiating treaties and contracts."

The Warden grunted. "It always comes down to money, doesn't it?"

The scope of the colony's wealth and influence became apparent as the *Ranger VII* joined the landing queue and entered the multihued Praxis Gargantua. Vast orbital ports and docking stations encircled the moon-sized asteroid of Cibola Seven. These bristled with dozens of anchored freighters and luxury ships, where holds were gorged with precious resources or passenger cabins expelled swarms of money-laden thrill-seekers and vacationers. Transports and shuttles moved in a steady ballet between the colony and these satellite stations to facilitate the transactions.

The asteroid itself glowed with brilliant strands of multicolored lights like holiday decorations beneath its wispy violet atmosphere. Though its surface never saw the light of any sun, Cibola Seven did not sleep.

Before landing, the Warden donned his form-fitting blue-and-silver spacesuit with its eye-concealing visor, and his belted twin Comet blaster pistols. Quantum was likewise armed and arrayed. They were not taking any chances, no matter how civilized Cibola Seven looked from several kilometers up.

The Warden and Quantum were met on their assigned orbital landing platform by the Chief Constable and two armed guards. The Chief Constable was a tall, dark-skinned, serious young man who was clearly not Maximo Ryan.

"Welcome to Cibola Seven, gentleman. I am Chief Constable Artemis Coppenger." His square jaw flinched through a smile as he shook hands. "Although we are honored to have the famous Last Star Warden as a guest, may I ask what brings you to our colony?"

The Warden matched Coppenger's forced smile. "We received a request for help from your predecessor. I take it Chief Ryan has been relieved of his duties?"

Coppenger tilted his short-cropped head. "Predecessor? I'm afraid I've held this office since the colony's founding, sir. And as for a… Chief Ryan? Well, I can honestly say I haven't the foggiest notion of whom you speak."

The Warden and Quantum exchanged glances. By all appearances, Coppenger wasn't much older than the colony of Cibola Seven.

"Perhaps this might help." Quantum raised his wrist chrono and tapped a button. A small rectangle of light hovered above the device, replaying the bizarre call for help.

Coppenger showed no visible sign of recognition. Or any other discernable reaction, for that matter. When the message concluded, he shrugged. "I have no explanation. However, feel free to look around if you like. When you get tired of chasing wild geese, you may find that Cibola Seven is a pleasant place to enjoy a little R&R. Judging by the stories I've heard since you first appeared on the Frontier, I'm guessing you could use some.

"If you like, I can introduce you to Mr. Tiberius Chen, the president of the C-7 Bank. I'm sure he would be more than happy to extend a line of credit to the Last Star Warden… and his companion."

The Warden nodded. "Thank you, but as soon as we're satisfied that this was a waste of time, we'll be on our way and out of your hair."

After Coppenger and his armed escort departed, the Warden and Quantum stood on the landing platform watching as people, luggage, and cargo moved back and forth along the busy decks.

"I have checked several times," Quantum said. "The message is not a forgery, and it did originate from this colony with a valid Alpha One priority code. The strange man in the video was wearing the same type of uniform as Mr. Coppenger, as well. It is... odd, to say the very least."

The Warden nodded. He watched the lines of people passing along the gangways. Those disembarking for their visit to Cibola Seven showed signs of fatigue, excitement, boredom, and every other normal trait associated with long-distance travel. Those making for the ships leaving the colony, however, displayed a variety of unusual quirks.

He saw people muttering to themselves, looking furtively over their shoulders as if being followed or harried by unseen threats, barely-contained sobs, near-maniacal laughter, and even a few unprovoked altercations that only failed to escalate because of the intervention of armed constables. One departing vacationer almost walked blithely into the jet wash of a launching shuttlecraft before being restrained by a safety bot.

"There is definitely something going on here, Quantum. We just need to find out what it is. I think we'd best start down on the asteroid itself."

Departing the shuttle bay on Cibola Seven's top tier, the Warden and Quantum stepped to the illuminated 3D directory. They entered Ryan's name and even fed the video footage of him into the database, but came up with no results.

"This is ridiculous." The Warden gritted his teeth, knotting his hands into fists.

Quantum looked at him. "Are you feeling unwell? I sense your blood pressure is slightly above normal and you seem unusually agitated by this minor setback."

The Warden took a deep breath and shook his head, scanning the passing crowds. "I'm fine. I just... I don't know. I can *feel* that something's not right here. I just can't put my finger on it. I guess we'll have to beat the bushes and see what we can flush out the old-fashioned way."

They spent the next three standard hours exploring various businesses and domiciles of Cibola Seven, asking questions and showing the missing chief's image. They were met with a wide variety of receptions—from warm and cheery, if confused, smiles to hostile suspicion and angry, foul language—but not a soul admitted to knowing anything at all about a Chief Constable Maximo Ryan or any other missing persons.

When, at the end of the three hours, yet another irritated Cibola citizen slammed the door in their faces, the Warden pounded the doorframe with his fist. "What the Sam Hill is going on here? If Ryan doesn't exist, then who sent that message? And why? Is this some sort of trap? If so, why haven't they sprung it yet? We've been chasing our tails long enough for a platoon of mercs or gang of pirates to ambush us at any time."

"We should take a break," Quantum said. "We both need sustenance, and I sense a growing frustration in you that could be deleterious to further investigations."

"*Deleterious*—! How could we do any worse?" The Warden sighed and slid his fingers under his visor to rub his eyes. "Sorry. There's just something about this case that's getting under my skin. I shouldn't take it out on you. You're right. Let's get something to eat."

Exiting the lift that opened onto the busy Restaurant and Eateries District, they made for a Senesian bistro across the way. The deck was crowded with off-duty, pub-hopping ship crews, vacationing couples who fancied themselves Galactic Foodies, and even a few local families out for dinner. Almost every race in the Civilized Worlds was represented somewhere among the crowds, and if not, they were certainly represented by one of the eating establishments.

Amid that galactic crowd, the Warden thought he recognized someone. Someone with dark hair and sparkling dark eyes. Someone he knew to be dead. Or as good as.

"Ramirez?"

He was yanked from this impossibility by a hand on his shoulder.

"Look." Quantum pointed down an alley between a hamburger joint and a Reticulan café. A large shadow crouched over another smaller one, arms rising and falling like violent pistons.

"Why is he doing this?" the attacking shadow roared. "How do I stop him?"

"Hey!" the Warden shouted. Shaking off his distraction, he launched into the darkened alley at a run. He tapped his visor to enhance illumination as the attacker sprang away at the sound of his approach. "Quantum, stay with the victim. I'll catch him."

The Warden gave chase, running down the narrow alleyway crowded with waste bins, empty packing crates, and various other refuse. It didn't take long to realize that the passage wasn't merely a space between two buildings but rather a single part of a much larger labyrinth of interconnected corridors. After losing sight of the attacker, the Warden couldn't even track him with thermal imaging due to the various kitchens venting into the alleyways. He soon found himself wandering around the maze for several more minutes before conceding the chase.

Raising his wrist chrono in frustration, he called Quantum. "He got away. Whoever he was, he moves fast for a big guy. Maybe boosted by cyberware or juice. Maybe an alien of some kind..."

When there was no response, the Warden felt a cold fist tighten around his gut. "Quantum? Are you there? Do you copy?"

He broke into a run, backtracking his footsteps until he came to the original alley's mouth. There was no sign of Quantum or the victim. Scanning the surrounding area, the Warden didn't see any indication of the initial struggle.

It was as if nothing had ever happened. And Quantum was gone.

The Warden looked back down the alley, then to the busy restaurant deck, where he thought he had seen Ramirez, the salvager who had died on that doomed space station in HPL-37. "Am I losing my mind...? What is going on here?"

Without another thought for food, he made straight for the Constabulary Office.

"I'm sorry, sir, you cannot go in there!" The prim and proper redheaded receptionist called as he brushed past her. He made straight for the big, antiquated oaken double doors of the inner office. "The Chief Constable is in a meeting of the First Five!"

"I don't care who he's meeting with. He is going to talk to me."

The Warden pushed the doors open and glared at the five individuals seated around a large, pentagonal table of polished black marble. A 3D hologram of five austere individuals hovered against the back wall, each person in the depiction a younger version of one of the five seated at the table—save for Coppenger, who looked like he had just posed for the image an hour before. These well-dressed scions looked at the Warden with something between concealed irritation and mild fascination.

"I'm sorry," the receptionist said. "He refused to listen—"

Coppenger stood. "Quite all right, Janet. I'm sure we'd all like to hear what the Last Star Warden has to say."

"I doubt that very much," the Warden said through clenched jaws. But he waited until the receptionist had departed and closed the doors.

"What can we do for you, Warden?" A heavyset man of Asian-Earth descent casually glanced at the gold pocket chrono he'd just withdrawn from his silken waistcoat. "It isn't every day that a living legend barges into a meeting of the First Five Citizens."

"I take it you're Mr. Chen?"

The man gave a smiling nod. "At your service. And I assume you've already met the Chief Constable. This is Augustus Sandoval, the president of the C-7 Mining Consortium, and these two young ladies are Ariadne Patel, the head of our operations fleet, and Portia Feldu, our esteemed mayor."

The Warden nodded at the overly polite introductions. Although the women were attractive for their apparent ages, Coppenger was the youngest of the group by at least two decades. "Pleased to meet you all. But I'm afraid there is something terribly wrong going on here. People are disappearing and no one seems to notice."

Coppenger raised an eyebrow. "Are you still on about this mysterious… Ryan, was it? I've already assured you, Warden, the man never existed."

"Really? Well, the same thing happened to my friend Quantum."

"Your friend?"

The Warden pounded his fists on the table. "Yes. The alien who accompanied me here. You met him just a few hours ago on the landing pad."

Coppenger frowned. "I'm sorry, Warden. But you were alone. Look…"

A holographic recording from a security camera appeared above the table. It clearly showed the Warden meeting with Coppenger and his armed retinue. Quantum was nowhere to be seen.

"That's… impossible."

"You don't look well, Warden," Mayor Feldu said with a pitying smile. "Let us help you. I'd be more than honored to put you up in a suite at the City of Gold hotel as my personal guest. You would not want for the least little thing, and we could have a medical bot sent to you in the most discreet of manners."

The Warden stiffened and looked at the blankly concerned faces. "Thank you. I am fine… I must have been mistaken. I apologize for the interruption."

Coppenger smiled, extended his arm to guide the Warden back to the doors. "Think nothing of it. It was our pleasure. And please, if you need anything, anything at all, don't hesitate to reach out to any one of us. We only want what is best for Cibola Seven, and that includes what is best for our guests."

The Warden nodded at the young man's deadpan smile.

Outside the Constabulary, the Warden started walking in a random direction. He was aware that no fewer than five constables were now following him while trying not to look like it. After changing directions and levels twice more, he raised this estimate to a dozen, half of which were plain-clothes or undercover operatives.

He was being watched.

"Perhaps going to the First Five wasn't the brightest idea. Now they know I'm onto whatever it is they're up to…" He stopped on a promenade and looked over a balcony at the throngs swimming between casinos and show bars. He realized he was looking for Ramirez in that crowd and shook his head. "Maybe I am cracking up… Just like Maximo Ryan…"

Realizing this was his only clue, the Warden went to a coffee house, slid into a secluded booth, and pulled up the recorded message on his chrono. He spent the next several standard hours drinking coffee and poring over every digitized detail. He magnified, enhanced, and extrapolated every frame until he finally found something.

In the background, when Ryan got up and walked around the room, for a split second a pink neon glow reflected on a picture frame. Ryan must have opened the curtains for a quick look, and in that moment the reflection of a sign was captured in the glass: ROXY'S ROCKETGIRLS.

Exhausted, his nerves frayed, the Warden at last had a starting point to begin his search for the missing Ryan. He could only hope this clue would eventually lead to finding Quantum, alive and well.

Based on the angle of reflection in the enhanced image, and the information gleaned from the colony's directory, he deduced that the room where the message was recorded should be on the seventh floor of the Get It Inn, across the street from the Roxy's Rocketgirls burlesque theater in the Red Light District.

It took two more hours for the Warden to give his watchers the slip before he could follow up on his lead…

The Red Light District was a multi-tiered conglomeration of brothels, skin shows, hourly motels, 4D arcades, streetwalkers, and body-bot boutiques. Just sharing the same atmosphere as the performers and their patrons made the Warden's skin crawl. He wasn't normally all that prudish, though he did have a certain level of disdain for the commercialized trivialization of intimacy. But something about the neon glare on the wet asphalt and the sickly sweet scent of perfume, pheromones, secretions, and incense hanging on the muggy air made him want to leave the nebula and never look back.

But he couldn't do that, would never do that. Not without Quantum.

They'd been through far too much together. Starting out as mortal enemies during the Continuum War, they had become the best of friends since being thrown into the far future. And while the Star Warden was a man out of time, he had to remind himself that Quantum was also a man out of space, trapped in this dimension with very little hope of ever seeing his home or loved ones again.

"And now, he's just gone." The Warden grunted as he stepped past the wet moaning sounds emanating from the alley outside the Get It Inn. Shaking his head, he entered the narrow building's lobby, thankful for the gloves and sealed spacesuit he wore.

"What's your pleasure, stranger?" The bored, pock-faced and frizzy-haired woman behind the counter chewed a lump of aphro-spice, smacking it against her too-red lips and ogling him with her too-shadowed eyes. "Looking for some company? 'Cause I can make that happen."

The Warden activated his chrono and brought up the image of Chief Ryan. "Official business. I'm looking for this man. I have good reason to believe he rented a room on the seventh floor less than a standard day ago."

The woman frowned, waved at the hologram. "Maybe. But that ain't no connie uniform you got on, stranger. Ain't no law on Cibola Seven but our own, so shove off or rent a room."

The Warden gnashed his teeth as he shut down the image. "How much for a room on the seventh floor?"

The woman smiled, smacked her spice again. "Now that's more like it, stranger.

You let me know if you get lonely up there…"

The Warden had no intention of using the procured room. Upon exiting the filthy lift on the seventh floor, he made his way to the front side of the building. He shouldered past amorous couples and trios bumping along the narrow corridors, headed for their rented lodgings.

Based upon the information he had extrapolated from Ryan's recorded message, the video had been made in one of three rooms. Using his visor's thermal imager, the Warden determined that one of these was occupied by a group of active individuals, another by a couple, and the third had a single occupant pacing relentlessly around the small bedroom.

The thermal readout indicated this occupant to be a large human male.

The Warden returned his visor to normal viewing and pressed the door's call button. "Chief Ryan? This is the Star Warden. I believe you called for my help."

The mechanical iris on the door's security loop opened. A raspy voice rattled through the dinged-up call system. "I don't believe you… You're an agent… an assassin… sent by… *him*!"

The Warden took a deep breath. He rested his hands on the hilts of his belted Comets. "I don't have time for this. You sent a message asking me to come and help you investigate murders and missing bodies. Well, I'm here and my friend has disappeared. So, either you open this door, or I blast it open."

The callbox squawked. The magnetic lock clunked in the door and it slid open. The haggard, hulking form of Maximo Ryan stood a meter on the other side, a heavy blaster pistol gripped in the gnarled and bloody fist at his side. The man looked even older than he had in the video message, his face grubbier, his eyes wilder and lined in dark circles.

"Come in." Ryan waved the blaster as an invitation or a command.

The Warden stepped in, keeping the strange man at arm's length and his hands near his own weapons. As soon as Ryan had secured the door, the Warden said, "All right. Start talking. What is going on here?"

Ryan's cracked and stubbled face broke into a disconcerting grin. "It *is* you. It's really you. You really came!" The big man shuddered, put his left hand to his watery eyes. "I can't believe you came. Thank the Cosmos, you came!"

The Warden scanned the room while Ryan regained his composure, or what was left of it. The small chamber smelled of body odor and spoiled food. The remnants of at least half a dozen takeaway meals occupied the surface of the two nightstands, the small table, and the foot of the unmade bed beside a portable computer. The digital device projected an elaborate display of glowing holographic images on the wall above the bed's headboard. The curtains were closed and the lights were out, the only other illumination from the floor lamps in the tiny, open lavatory.

"Who were you talking about?" The Warden turned his attention back to the armed madman. "Who did you think sent me? What did you mean by *him*?"

Ryan uttered a bitter cluck of laughter and moved to the window. Giving a furtive glance through the heavy purple curtains, he said, "The God of Cibola. He controls everything here. He controls us. And, I think—I think he is going mad... Just like the rest of us..."

The Warden gnashed his teeth, fighting down the urge to disarm Ryan and throttle him until he started making sense. He shook his head, trying to clear his own thoughts. *I'm tired and frustrated. I'm worried about Quantum, and I can't help but feel like I've already failed him. Already lost him...*

Ryan turned from the window, the blaster still in his hand. "When you chased me in the alley, I thought they had sent you. The First Five, the Fist of the Mad God..." He chuckled and licked his lips. "Yes, I quite like that, *The Fist of the Mad God*. Nice turn of phrase, that..."

The Warden raised his chin. "That was you in the alley? That man you attacked, who was he? Why did you attack him?"

Ryan's mirth vanished in swift, fiery eyed rage. "That was no man! He was an agent for the God of Cibola! He was following me, wanted to find me here with all my evidence. He would have killed me and taken it to them, the Five, to secure their little conspiracy... Well, I say *little*, but they have the entire galaxy by the throat with their control of the lithium... And the Mad God controls them..."

The Warden glanced at the array of digital images projected against the wall. He saw news stories, public photos of the First Five Citizens—including Maximo Ryan, himself, group photos, shipping manifests, credit reports, crime reports, and personnel files connected by glowing strands of red light. All these bits of information radiated outward like a spider's web from an image of The Old Number One Mine.

A honking warble from the street below drew Ryan's attention back to the window.

"The constables!" Ryan turned to face the Warden, his hate-filled face lined in pink neon. "You led them to me!" He raised his blaster.

The Warden drew his own weapons. "No! They must have followed me without my knowledge!"

Ryan fired.

As did the Warden.

In the span of a heartbeat, the darkened room blazed with galvanized plasma. Ryan's hulking body slammed into and through the window, dragging the heavy curtains with it to the wet pavement seven stories below.

The Warden stood in the filthy room, now awash in the glow of pink and purple neon. His Comets smoking in his hands, he saw that Ryan had not aimed at him, but at the now destroyed computer deck which had projected the gathered images on the wall.

The madman had only been trying to cover his tracks. Trying to protect his secrets.

"I tried to warn him… Didn't I?" The Warden shook with guilt and uncertainty. He looked at the weapons in his hands, despising the lethal training which had made him so fast, so accurate.

Shouted orders from the street below broke his stupor. Holstering his pistols, the Warden bolted from the room. He knew the constables would be watching the elevator in the lobby, and at least one fire team would be swarming up each of the two stairwells. He ran for the nearest stairs and headed for the roof.

Bursting into the relatively fresh, misty air, the Warden was blasted by the searchlight from a constabulary tactical shuttle. Six armored constables fast-roped onto the roof from the hovering vehicle. A loudspeaker warbled something about surrender and arrest.

The Warden charged into the descending constables, catching the first man before he could disengage from his roped harness. Sweeping his legs from under him, the Warden slammed the constable to the ground and punched him in the throat, between his helmet and vest.

Leaping from the downed man, he drove his elbow into the armored solar plexus of the next officer. Grabbing the winded constable's arm, the Warden twisted, flipping him into the next man in line.

The Warden knew he could use his Comets to end this fight in a hurry. But after killing Ryan, he couldn't bring himself to touch the weapons. Whatever else was going on here, these constables were just doing their job.

A job they were good at, apparently. After his initial success, it didn't take long for the remainder of the team to surround him and hit him with stun weapons. The Warden shuddered under the blast of neural-disrupting charges, his consciousness slipping away as painful spasms ripped through his body...

The Warden woke in pain. He opened his eyes and stared through the scratched lens of his visor, felt waves of soreness in his arms, back, chest, and neck. When he sat up, he realized the worst of the agony nested in his skull.

He groaned.

"You're awake." A woman's voice from the shadows. "Earlier than I expected."

The Warden turned in the direction of the words, tapped his visor, waited for the pixelated image to resolve in enhanced illumination. He thought he was dead.

Or at the very least, communing with the dead.

An olive-skinned woman sat in a swivel chair at the controls of a small shuttlecraft. The pale glow of the nebula outside the forward screen limned her utility spacesuit and dark hair in shades of violet and pink.

She looked very much like Ramirez.

"Who are you? Where are we?" The Warden rubbed the bruises on his arms and shoulders, trying to convince himself of the reality of his situation. He noted that his holsters were empty but felt only a sense of relief at this observation. Checking his chrono, he noted that he'd been out for about three standard hours. "What happened?"

The woman got up and fetched a med-kit from the shuttle's wall. "I'm Maria Sandoval. My father runs the mining operation." She knelt beside him, fishing out a hypo-syringe from the kit. "Here, this will boost your body's regenerative abilities. I didn't want to dose you while you were out. Sometimes unconsciousness can turn into a coma with these old nanites."

The Warden grunted, studying the lean lines of her face. Just like Ramirez, she was pretty, in her early thirties, with a sharp look in her dark eyes. "You're... helping me? I should be in custody, locked away somewhere beneath the constabulary right now. Or worse."

Maria smiled as she administered the hypo. "Probably. But I've been following your movements since you arrived on Cibola Seven, and as soon as I heard a tac-team was dispatched to bring you in, I conned my way into piloting the prisoner transport. I was able to get you off the colony, but I couldn't do much about the beating the connies gave you while you were down. Apparently, they didn't like the way you resisted arrest."

The Warden nodded, rubbed his face with his hands. He was relieved by her confession of following him. At least he wasn't seeing dead people. But that didn't change the fact that he had just killed the man he had come to Cibola Seven to help. "No less than I deserve..."

He couldn't shake the image of Maximo Ryan's wild-eyes staring at him as he blasted him out of that dingy flophouse room. The madman seemed to move in slow motion as the fiery plasma bolts hit him in the chest, lifted him from the floor, and hurled him through the window. Ryan's face was blank, emotionless. That lack of accusation, of any sense of betrayal was even worse than if there had been a look of hatred in his eyes.

The Warden cleared his throat. "Off the colony? So where are we? And why are you doing this? Shouldn't you be part of your father's conspiracy? Aren't you the legacy of the First Five Citizens?"

Maria shrugged and stood to pace the small cabin. "Something's... not right on Cibola Seven. It just started a few weeks ago, but I think it's getting worse. And fast... People have gone missing, and I don't mean just disappearing." She fixed him with a frightened look. "I mean it's as if they never existed. Nobody, not even their family and friends remember them. And somehow, they're even wiped from the databases and registries... I'm terrified."

The Warden nodded. "You lost someone?"

Maria rubbed her brow. "My... fiancé or husband. I think; I can't be sure... I wake up sometimes, knowing that someone should be in the bed beside me, but there isn't... For the briefest of moments, I can see him smiling at me or snoring at the ceiling. I can smell him, feel his warmth..."

She wiped at her left eye and fixed the Warden with a resolute glare. "And then... he's just gone. But I *know* in my bones that he was there. I know it. And when I get away from Cibola Seven for a while, I can sometimes... catch actual memories..."

The Warden pulled himself to his feet and limped to the copilot seat at the controls. He stared through the forward screen, scanned the readouts on the nav computer. "We're on a smaller asteroid in the belt, several thousand kilometers from the main colony. You obviously brought me out here for a reason. What's your plan?"

Maria sat down beside him and shook her head. "I honestly don't know. I hoped you'd have one."

The Warden thought about Ryan's evidence, the data he had given his life to protect from whatever conspiracy was at the heart of this mystery. "What do you know about The Old Number One Mine?"

Maria's brow wrinkled. "It's been closed down for over a decade. Mined out. It was the first shaft we dug when we got here... Now that I think on it, as far back as I can remember, even when I was a kid, it was always under heavy guard. Only crews hand-picked by my dad ever worked it, and most of the actual mining was done by bots... Why do you ask?"

"I believe we might find some answers in there. Is there any way you can get us in?"

Maria smiled. "Maybe. But it won't be easy."

The Warden grudgingly returned the smile. For the first time since arriving on Cibola Seven, he didn't feel a nagging sense of irritation bordering on violent rage.

"Nothing worth doing is ever easy."

The Old Number One Mine occupied the lowest level of the colony. In just over two decades, a hole in the asteroid's surface had been buried beneath sixteen layers of residential communities, business districts, and entertainment and commerce zones, as well as industrial sectors for refineries, storehouses, shipyards, and manufacturing plants. And though there were other mining operations on the primary asteroid, the original shaft now sat at the heart of a security complex the Warden thought would have put some military facilities to shame.

"I hope you know what you're doing." The Warden rubbed the bruise on his chin as Maria guided the shuttle down the deep well that would lead them to the Old

Number One.

"Don't worry." She cast him a nervous smile. "Even if I didn't know my dad's passwords, I could still slide the security systems. He's one of the best miners in the Frontier, but he never was too savvy on computers or technology."

The Warden returned the smile. "Well, that makes two of us."

An alarm on the control panel alerted them to a weapons lock.

Maria tapped a sequence of code and the alarm ended. An automated voice came over the coms: "Shuttle Twelve, you are cleared for landing on Pad Nine."

"What are we going to do when we're met by a squad of security bots?"

Maria shook her head and typed more code. "We won't be. I'm telling them to stand down now."

"Let's just hope they don't have any bored rent-a-cops on duty."

She frowned. "Are you always this negative?"

The Warden chuckled. "It's a recent development."

They were not met by a security detail of any sort.

"This way." Maria led him off the landing pad and across a short, graveled yard to a sealed concrete bunker.

The Warden noted the array of security cameras documenting their every move. "What about those?"

Maria ignored him and entered a code on the blast door's keypad. She knelt and placed her face near the retina scanner. A few moments later the display turned green and the heavy doors slid open. "We're in."

They hurried down a short, low corridor to a service lift. Boarding it, Maria pressed the button for the lowest level. A moment later they zipped toward the heart of the mine, the asteroid, and Cibola Seven.

The Warden suddenly felt naked without his Comets. "We should have brought weapons."

Maria glanced at him and held up her chrono. "I can disable any bots we come across. And do you really want to shoot anybody? Considering I know you were armed when the connies took you into custody and you didn't draw your weapons, I'm guessing not."

The Warden grunted. "I never *want* to shoot anybody. But when they shoot at me, it's usually the only option left."

Maria grunted back.

The doors opened onto a pitch-black corridor filled with a strange scent, both chemical and earthy. The Warden had to tap his visor twice to get it to switch to low-light vision. "Those constables did a number on my electronics. Wish something could fix them as quickly as the nanites did my skull."

"Quiet." Maria shushed him. She slid on a pair of goggles to augment her own vision. Crouching, she led him out of the elevator with a whisper. "I think I hear someone down here."

They crept along the earthen tunnel for several meters before coming to a bend that twisted and descended to the left. They could clearly hear a single male voice echoing faintly from below. The Warden stepped past Maria and quietly led her into an opening that was the terminus of six narrow tunnels descending deeper into the asteroid. They made their way to the mouth of the tunnel from which the voice emanated.

Maria touched her chrono to the Warden's, then typed a quick message. It displayed on his: *That is my father.*

He nodded and they moved into the tunnel. It twisted and continued to descend until coming to another opening. This one was the T-junction with another shaft. At the center of this intersection stood a small, GlasSteel prefab office or administration building. The Warden recognized Augustus Sandoval sitting in the booth, hands resting on his knees as he stared into space while speaking to someone.

The Warden typed onto his chrono: *Does he have retinal or subdural communication implants?*

Maria read the message and shook her head.

The Warden looked again, trying to see if the mining magnate was using some kind of technical device for communication. The man obviously wasn't using his wrist chrono, and there were no discernible mechanisms in the booth, only outdated monitors and keyboards and a dusty locker marked TORCHES & DIGGERS.

After a moment, Sandoval blinked and looked in their direction. Jumping to his feet, he spoke into his chrono. The entire darkened complex erupted in red flashing light and blaring sirens.

Before the Warden and Maria had time to turn and run, a swarm of armed security bots surrounded them. Maria tried to use her codes, but to no avail.

As the sirens quieted and the red strobes were replaced with the subdued white glow of auxiliary lighting, the Warden and Maria were escorted to face Augustus Sandoval.

"What is going on here, Dad?" Maria said. "Why are you down here alone, and who were you talking to?"

The elder Sandoval blinked as if trying to recognize her. "I don't know who you two are, but I've far more business down here than either of you."

Maria's eyes went wide and her jaw dropped. "Dad...?"

"Look here, Sandoval," the Warden said. "You are up to something and I want to know what it is. Where is my friend Quantum? What have you people done with him?"

Augustus looked at him for the first time with recognition and smiled. "Why, Warden, I'm so glad you came to visit our operation. It is my greatest pleasure to show it to you. I think you'll be quite impressed with what we have going on here. It has made a ragtag bunch of Undocs the wealthy envy of the entire galaxy in less than half a lifetime."

"Dad! What are you talking about?"

Augustus Sandoval blinked at his daughter again, frowning as if he'd forgotten something very important. Clearing his throat, he said, "I'm talking about the greatest discovery any mortal being in this universe has ever made. In the heart of this asteroid, at the bottom of this mine, two decades ago, we found God.

"And now you get to meet Him."

Sandoval led them deeper into the mine. The Warden and Maria were not bound, but instead were surrounded by a dozen armored security bots.

The lighting grew dim as they descended into the oldest parts of the shaft. The smell of earth and chemicals gradually faded into the stench of unclean bodies and warm electronics. A strange, almost hypnotic hum filled the thin air, echoing off the close rock walls.

Rounding a corner, they found the source of these sensations, or at least a part of it. A thin, middle-aged woman stood strapped to the rugged wall by a strange metallic harness. Though she appeared to be in no pain, she stared slack jawed and blank-eyed from the illuminated apparatus enclosing her head.

Maria gasped, but the Warden's eyes followed the cables running from the harness farther down the corridor. It was connected to another trapped, catatonic individual, this one a slender young man. They passed three more such captives before they came to Quantum.

"Tarnation!" The Warden stepped to his friend, grasped the Mechtechan's narrow shoulders and stared into his blank black eyes. "Quantum! Speak to me! Are you all right?"

Sandoval frowned. "He cannot hear you, Warden. He is in communion with God at the moment, free from all worldly concerns, including you. But do not fret, you will be joining him in this sacred bond very shortly."

The Warden shook with rage. "If you've hurt him, so help me, I'll kill you all and burn this Sodom to the ground around your blasted corpses."

Sandoval smiled, shook his head, and continued down the tunnel.

Two of the bots grasped the Warden by the shoulders and pushed him forward.

The Warden looked back at Quantum, then turned to stare at the back of Sandoval's head. The irrational rage he'd felt since his arrival on the asteroid was very near the surface now, threatening to escape his control. He knew he could reach out and snap the man's neck before the bots could get off a shot.

It took every iota of his willpower not to do it.

Sandoval was oblivious to all this as he led them into a larger chamber filled with a pale green glow. The circular room's walls were lined with more people wired in "communion." Maria recognized someone on the far side of the room.

With a cry of, "Marcus!", she ran to the inert man, tried to embrace him, and fell weeping at his feet.

The Warden felt for her, but his attention was arrested by the terminus of the macabre network. The center of the room was occupied by a large mechanical throne of dull black metal.

Upon the chair sat the source of the pale green glow, the God of Cibola.

The tall, gaunt Tuatha was a creature of living plasma, its body merely a construct

of energized atoms drawn from the surrounding atmosphere to sheathe the ever-living consciousness of one of the oldest beings in the galaxy. Possibly even the universe. In fact, according to common belief, it should not exist at all. This was probably the last of its kind.

Sandoval bowed formally, though the seated Tuatha showed no indication that it was aware of their arrival. Turning to the Warden, the mining magnate said, "Behold the face of God, Warden. Are you not humbled? Should you not kneel before your Creator?"

The Warden glanced at the man. "You idiot. That's not God. That's a Tuatha, one of the original inhabitants of the Frontier. What the hell have you lot done to it?"

Ignoring Sandoval's incensed sputtering, the Warden stepped forward and made a gesture he had learned a long time ago. Years before the Star Wardens had fallen in the Continuum War against the Mechtechan, they had fought the Tuatha and eventually forged a peace with the ancient race. They had reached an accord, dividing Frontier Space between the powerful aliens and the burgeoning United Planetary Council.

Since his return to the timeline, however, the Warden had learned that the U.P.C. had broken the peace. Trusting in the might of their vaunted Star Cav, the United Planets had invaded the ceded systems, starting a new Tuatha War. A war that had ultimately ended with the Tuatha choosing their own extinction rather than fighting a war that could only end in mass genocide on a galactic level.

The Warden's gesture of greeting seemed to catch the enthroned and catatonic Tuatha's attention. Its glowing, featureless head turned in his direction. A moment later, its consciousness entered his mind. The sensation took his breath, drove him to his knees. In an instant he knew all that had transpired to lead them to this point in time...

The Warden saw the Tuatha's scientific research vessel enter the Praxis Gargantua hundreds of years ago. He saw it struck by asteroids, forcing it to crash on what would eventually become Cibola Seven. He saw the Tuatha, named Belgu, go deep underground to find protection from the nebula's particles that disrupted its physical form. He saw it gradually lose hope of being rescued before its resources failed. He watched as Belgu entered a stasis field and slept for centuries...

He saw the faces of the First Five Citizens as young explorers and colonists when they discovered the hibernating Belgu. A young Maximo Ryan was among them, but not the handsome Artemis Coppenger. The Warden saw the grateful Tuatha form a partnership with this group of harried Undocs. He watched as Belgu guided them with psychic wisdom and helped to improve their technology as they built the mining empire that would make Cibola Seven a powerhouse on the Frontier and throughout the galaxy.

But then the images grew dark and murky. Belgu began to hear rumors and stories from the various visitors to Cibola Seven. It learned of a war... a war between the United Planets and its own people. It heard rumors that its own kind no longer existed. So Belgu set out to discover the truth. But, just as before, when it had first crashed on the asteroid, Belgu found it difficult to signal beyond the nebula's interference.

Belgu needed more psychic energy. It needed "boosters."

And so, the Tuatha used its influence over the First Five to acquire those boosters from among the populace and the visitors of Cibola Seven. Maximo Ryan, in his role as Chief Constable, was Belgu's prime accomplice in this operation. But as the booster network grew and Belgu still could find no others of its kind with which to telepathically connect, it grew desperate and depressed.

The Tuatha's powerful mind began to fill with the fear and confusion of the many,

many people it now used for psychic energy. This fear and confusion began to feed on itself.

Belgu began to lose focus. It began to lose control. The Tuatha could feel its own unsettled emotions and concerns seeping out, washing over the asteroid's inhabitants, affecting them. Belgu tried harder, requiring more boosters, which in turn only exacerbated the situation.

And then Maximo Ryan began to have his doubts, began to question his actions. When the Chief Constable confronted it, Belgu wiped his mind and tried to force him into a harness, but Ryan proved too strong and fled raving into the city to be lost in madness. But the Tuatha quickly found a new catspaw in the ambitious Coppenger.

By now, Belgu had mastered the art of manipulating and altering digital imagery and computer code. To a being as old as the Tuatha, what difference did a few decades make to chronology...?

The Warden gulped in the foul air as strong metallic hands pulled him to his feet. He blinked, free of the alien thoughts and memories. The security bots hauled him and Maria to new harnesses being wired into the booster network.

Sandoval stood smiling beside the vacant places. "You are so very lucky, Warden. You and your young companion will now know the eternal joy of becoming one with God."

"Belgu!" the Warden shouted. "The rumors are true. You are the last of your kind. The Tuatha destroyed themselves decades ago. They are all gone. You will never reach them, no matter how many people you drag down here and wire into your mind. All you will accomplish is driving yourself irrevocably insane while destroying the lives of countless others.

"I thought the Tuatha were a civilized people!"

The green glow of the seated being of energy pulsed and shifted along the spectrum until it became a brilliant scarlet fire. A moment later, waves of hatred and rage rippled through the Warden's mind, followed immediately by exquisite agony. He almost didn't hear the horrific cries of the people wired into the network over his own hoarse exclamations and the surprised wails of Maria and her father.

Crumpled on the cavern floor, gasping for breath as his head threatened to explode, the Warden's heart was crushed under the weight of a loneliness and isolation he thought he could never imagine.

Somewhere, deep within his rupturing psyche, he understood that loneliness was the key.

Belgu! Unable to articulate comprehensible speech, the Warden reached out with his mind, trying to reconnect the psychic link he had shared with the Tuatha. Unsure if he had succeeded or not, he forced himself to ignore the pain that systematically shredded his existence, and to focus on his friendship with Quantum, and on the people he had met and helped since his return to the timeline.

You don't have to be alone. There are good people in this galaxy. People with whom you can form relationships. People with whom you can build a new life. And as long as you are alive, some part of your people, your loved ones, will live on in you. Please, Belgu. Please release us and choose to live. Do not let the Tuatha die down in this hole...

The Warden blinked, suddenly aware of the absence of pain.

He struggled to his feet and looked around. The boosters were sleepily emerging from their harnesses, looking around in confusion. Maria and her father shared a tearful embrace with the man she had called Marcus.

The Warden turned to head back up the tunnel to where he knew Quantum would be escaping his own comatose captivity. But he was frozen by a rush of emotion and the sensation of renewed energy at the room's center. He turned back to the Tuatha.

Belgu had risen from its throne, glowing a peaceful aqua color as it stood before him. The Warden heard its voice in his mind, more focused and articulate than before.

I am sorry for the harm I have done here. As soon as I entered this device and connected with the first alien mind, I was no longer truly myself. I was no longer Tuatha... I fed my own doubts and fears with those of the people I sought to use for my experiment... Thank you for freeing me from my own folly. My own madness.

The Warden cleared his sore throat. "It was foolishness. It was madness. But I can understand what drove you to do it... And I am sorry that the organization I once served did what they did to your people..." He thought of Maximo Ryan. "I have my own regrets. Mistakes were made… Tragic ones…"

The Tuatha tilted its glowing head toward the ceiling. *Yes. Mistakes were made on all sides… But you are right. We must all choose to be the civilized people we hope to be, even if we are not there just yet.*

Augustus and Maria Sandoval drew near, supporting the dazed Marcus between them. The miner stared at the Tuatha, but gone was the servile reverence of moments before. "You are… Belgu. You helped us build Cibola Seven… and then you did *this*."

Belgu nodded, its thoughts touching all present. *Yes, I have erred. But if it is at all possible, I hope to make restitution for my actions. To that end, I will return to my home world and see if there is some positive aspect of my people's culture which I might cultivate and share with the galaxy… That is, unless you think I should be punished for my transgressions here…*

Maria hugged her husband tighter and glanced at the Warden. "I'm sure there's been a crime of some kind committed, but as we say on Cibola Seven, we recognize no law but our own. As for me, I'm just glad to have my family back… I don't have any room in my heart for vengeance now."

The Warden looked around at the confused but unharmed people now being ministered to by the security bots. "I wouldn't even know where to begin with such a case… Unless I learn otherwise, *I* was the only one to actually kill someone in all this mess."

Belgu shifted to a softer hue of blue. *You and Maximo Ryan were both under the influence of my madness at the time. You were drawn into this scenario against your will. You should not hold yourself responsible.*

The Warden shrugged, looked at his gloved hands. "He's still dead."

As are my people… Should we seek justice for that, or can we not acknowledge it for the tragedy that it is? Can we not try to move forward and make the galaxy a better place, having learned from the experience? Tell me, can you not move forward, having learned from this?

The Warden took a deep breath and nodded. "Still, I should face Cibola Seven's justice. I should stand trial."

Augustus Sandoval shook his head. "Warden, look around. If you hadn't come here, hadn't kept digging for the truth, there is no telling what we would have done to ourselves. The First Five Citizens, including myself *and* Ryan, were far more culpable in any wrongdoing than you... There is no justice, no punishment to be had here save what we have already inflicted on ourselves. I'm sure you can understand that?"

The Warden grunted, knowing he would spend the rest of his life punishing himself for the death of Maximo Ryan. He looked down the corridor and saw the familiar lanky silhouette of Quantum staggering into the chamber. He nodded to the Sandoval family and to the Tuatha.

"Best of luck to you all. Right now, it looks like I've got a friend who could use a hand."

Quantum met the Warden with a weak, confused grin. "I understand what has transpired, due to my psychic connection with the Tuatha... I am... I am glad you did not forget about me as so many others were forgotten."

The Warden slapped him on the back with a relieved smile. "I could never do that, my friend. Come on, what say we go get that bite to eat now?"

ESCAPE FROM HULK 13

"**W**hat've you got?" the Last Star Warden asked as he drifted into the *Ranger VII*'s command chair.

Quantum's antennae twirled. Pulling up a display on the forward view screen, he said, "Does this look familiar?"

The Warden stared at the enormous void slowly devouring a distant system. He nodded, feeling a cold fist close around his gut. He saw the singularity not as it was at that moment, but as it had been over a century before: the battlefield of the largest interdimensional invasion in recorded history. At least in this universe. He saw men and ships consumed in fiery conflagrations as the hulking Mechtechan cruisers emerged from the event horizon, particle cannons blazing.

"It does. Frontier Singularity One. What about it?"

"Since our time, it has been given a new name: Draconus Prime." Quantum turned to face him. The Mechtechan's big, expressionless black eyes did not blink, and his undersized mouth showed no hint of emotion. "What if I told you I think I can use it to open a wormhole back to the time of the battle?"

The Warden's jaw dropped. "I'd say being wired up to that Tuatha scrambled your egg. Why in the worlds would you ever want to do that?"

"We could return to our own time. Our own people."

The Warden inhaled. It had not been easy, but he had finally come to grips with his place in this new era. Clearly Quantum's recent and traumatic sojourn on Cibola Seven had not had the same result. "I'm sorry you're the only Mechtechan left in this reality, my friend… But that's just too dangerous to even comprehend. Even if you could do such a thing, what are the odds your people wouldn't take advantage and launch a new invasion?"

Quantum turned back to the ship's controls. "They were defeated by your relatively small force of Wardens over a century ago. The United Planetary Council now has several fleets of more impressive ships in its Star Cav. That should prove deterrent enough.

"Besides, if my calculations are correct, I could actually open a one-way portal for each of us..."

"*If*—? What calculations? What are you basing this on?"

Quantum glanced at him. "I kept the data gathered on the station in HPL-37. I've been constructing theoretical models ever since. And while connected to the impressive mind of the Tuatha, I was able to make some valuable insights into the specifics of the multi-dimensional superstring geometry involved in such an undertaking."

The Warden closed his eyes and shook his head. There were too many nightmares associated with that accursed space station and with the Cibola Seven case, and now Quantum wanted to use those hellish experiences for this new madness. The casual nature with which Quantum proposed the idea bothered the Warden in a deep and surprising way. It was as if there were suddenly an aspect to his friend's personality he had yet discovered—a cold, detached, and unsettling one.

A blaster bolt arced past the forward viewport as the proximity alarms sounded.

"We're under attack." Quantum's observation was as unemotional as it was unnecessary. "By four assault craft. Star Cav by their ident codes."

The Warden grabbed the controls and pushed the *Ranger VII* into a high-speed evasive maneuver. "What in the Sam Hill does Star Cav want with us?"

Quantum opened the coms to the attacking ship's hail. "*Attention, Star Warden. This is Lt. Commander Drake of the* S.C.S.S. *Oreto. You are under arrest by the authority of the United Planetary Council for violation of Star Law. Stand down and surrender or we will destroy your ship.*"

The Warden glanced at the sensor readouts, checked the distance to the closest Einstein-Rosen bridge, and did the math. "There's no way we can outrun those fast-attack ships. They'll cut us off before we can make it to an ERB."

"We could fight," Quantum offered, his hand hovering over the weapons system controls. "If we disable one or two, we increase the odds of escape. But we will have to strike fast and decisively."

The Warden powered down the ship's engines. "I'm not fighting Star Cav without a very good reason. Besides, maybe they're right. Maybe I am guilty of breaking Star Law."

Quantum's antennae flicked. "I believe the incident to which you refer was a clear case of self-defense, or as the officials on Cibola Seven declared it, Justifiable Homicide. You were exonerated."

The Warden didn't completely agree. He knew he would be haunted by the mad, tortured eyes of Maximo Ryan for the rest of his days, no matter what timeline he occupied.

He activated the coms. "This is the Warden. We surrender."

Lt. Commander Drake's voice responded. "*Prepare to be taken in tow. We will escort you to Hulk 13 for processing. If you attempt to power up your weapons or engines, we will destroy you.*"

"Understood."

Closing the channel, the Warden turned to Quantum. "They're not boarding us. That's odd... And Hulk 13? Isn't that the prison ship that keeps a constant irregular course on the outskirts of the Frontier?"

Quantum nodded. "Yes. Once the largest warship built during the Tuatha Wars, the *S.C.S.S. Arioch* was later decommissioned and re-designated as a prison for war criminals and deserters. Soon after, Hulk 13 was privatized when the U.P.C. turned over all penal facilities to corporate interests.

"In the ensuing years, as its size and inmate population grew, it gained a somewhat nefarious reputation as the worst place in the galaxy. I believe it is commonly referred to as the 'Ship of the Damned' or the 'Hell Ship.'"

"A simple 'yes' would have sufficed."

Commandant Stanislaus King stood before the wall-sized 3D painting of *The Battle of Draconus Prime* hanging in his office. The scintillating, ever-changing two-meter by five-meter image depicted the climactic battle between the Star Wardens and the invading Mechtechan battle fleet. It had been painted by the master Roan Melrose almost a century ago and was now worth over six years of King's salary.

But King had paid only a fraction of that sum to have the painting's previous owner framed for a crime. A crime which would have consigned the man to prison—King's prison—for a lifetime. The man, a high-ranking corporate officer, was more than willing to part with *The Battle of Draconus Prime* to secure his continued freedom.

King always got what he wanted, at least regarding his private passion. He had grown up on stories and legends surrounding the fabled Star Wardens. But by the time he was an adult, the once great service had fallen into disfavor and scandal. Still, being a man of action with a taste for adventure, he had joined Star Cav and risen through the ranks with honor.

For a while, at least.

He had never forgotten about those brave souls in the silvery sleek Ranger-class ships blasting into the uncharted dark, mapping the Frontier, protecting intrepid colonists, battling unknown foes, and enforcing peace in a lawless expanse of space. In truth, he was obsessed with them, and had come to be one of the leading authorities on not only the Wardens themselves, but also on the epic conflict with the Mechtechan, which had ultimately been their undoing.

Of course, that was not saying much nowadays. Few cared to recall an old-fashioned and disgraced organization, much less put forth the time and effort in its study. The Star Wardens were a thing best left in the past, a naïve and romantic endeavor from a simpler, more prosaic time. They had no place in the modern worlds and the harsh Frontier of today.

Though the Star Wardens had won the Continuum War, had driven the Mechtechan back to their own dimension and saved this one, it was a pyric victory. Their numbers and resources were so depleted that the United Planetary Council lowered standards to quickly rejuvenate the decimated Wardens. Quantity had replaced quality, inviting corruption and abuse of power, thus ensuring the speedy end of the once great agency.

A chirp at the office door stirred King from his reverie. "Come."

"Excuse me, Commandant." Ilsa Braun, King's first officer, stepped through the sliding door. Like King, the tall blonde wore a crisp military-style grey uniform and polished jackboots. "We just received word from the task force. They have secured the target and are on their way to the ERB. They should be at the rendezvous in less than half a standard hour."

King inhaled sharply. He appreciated Braun's loyalty and skillful performance of her tasks, but the way her womanly curves imposed on the fabric of her martial attire bothered him. "Very good. Have Jericho meet us in the docking bay with a detachment in heavy riot gear."

Braun snapped to attention and gave a crisp bow before departing to carry out the order. King watched her go and gave a grudging smile. She may be a woman, he mused, but she certainly knows her place. "Most underlings would have questioned why such a heavy guard was required. But then, perhaps my idle observations have imparted to her some understanding of the dangers posed by Star Wardens and the Mechtechan."

"Those are not Star Cav ships."

The Warden looked out the forward view port as they passed through the space-folding field of the Einstein-Rosen bridge. The brilliant coils of multi-hued energy spiraling around the spacecraft seemed to shimmer and glow in bright patches through the escorting ships. As he stared, the Warden saw the illusion of the Star Cav assault craft become transparent, revealing the grungy and irregular fuselages of private vessels. "Hologram cloaks."

"Bounty hunters. It would seem we have been duped." Again, Quantum's lack of emotion unsettled the Warden. "Though I am unable to find any record of a bounty on either of us in the usual channels."

The Warden pushed himself through the hatch leading to the crew quarters. "Well, there's no way out of this now, in any case. I guess we just have to wait and see who hired them and for what purpose."

Pulling on his spacesuit, the Warden was glad Quantum had not pointed out that his suggestion to fight had been the right decision. On second thought, however, he realized that a human companion would have most likely done so, if even in jest.

But jesting was one thing Quantum rarely ever did. At least not intentionally.

Donning his multi-spectrum visor, the Warden glanced into the cockpit and watched as his Mechtechan friend locked down the *Ranger VII*'s controls. The two of them had been through so much together, more than probably any other pair of comrades in the entire galaxy. They had met as enemies in the heat of battle, but an unexpected act of humanity had made them allies while a vagary of interdimensional physics had thrust them through a hole in space and time.

They had faced the Continuum War, pirates, corporate mercenaries, alien overlords, and even rips in the fabric of reality itself. They had stood shoulder-to-shoulder and back-to-back in firefights and fistfights, had pulled each other out of burning ships and the vacuum of space, and had encouraged each other through the slow times, the hard times of isolation and separation that only comes from being the last of your generation or your species in a vast new universe.

And yet, for all that, there was still a rift between them. A cavernous gulf that separated them, manifested in a million tiny differences: Quantum's vastly superior intellect and heightened senses which often made the Warden feel like a stupid child, the way Quantum never got the Warden's jokes or personal references but sometimes knew what he was about to say before he said it, Quantum's dislike of most human foods, the strange alien music he sometimes played that hurt the Warden's head for hours afterward, the way Quantum slept standing up with his eyes open, and even the fact that the Warden couldn't pronounce Quantum's actual name without getting a nosebleed. These were constant reminders that the Warden's best and only friend in the galaxy was an alien from another dimension who had, at one time, nearly killed him.

"We've just spent too much time locked up together on this ship is all." The Warden sighed and shook his head as he strapped on his gun belt.

"So, where are these bounty hunters really taking us?" The Warden asked as he returned to the bridge.

Quantum looked at him. "It appears that we are indeed rendezvousing with Hulk 13."

A moment later, the small convoy of ships exited the Einstein-Rosen bridge, emerging into normal space in a flash of black light. The Warden looked through the forward view port and saw the massive prison ship lumbering toward them. Nowhere near as big as the SuperCorp Sun Smasher, the ancient hulk somehow seemed twice as menacing.

In the decades since being decommissioned as a warship, the Hulk had grown as new wings and compartments had been added to house the ever-growing prison population. The profile of the thing now looked more like some misshapen hornet's nest than a sleek ship of the line. Bulbous, windowless protrusions seemed to grow out of the spacecraft's hull like leprous scabs or tumors, while gun towers stood at odd angles to provide as much intimidation as defense.

"I've never seen an uglier ship in all my life."

"If we do not come up with a solution, it is entirely possible that it will be the last ship we ever see."

The bounty hunters veered off as soon as the Hulk 13's docking beams locked onto the *Ranger VII*. They had been paid to deliver the ship and its crew and were not hanging around to see how things turned out. Without so much as another communique, the four ships made straight for the ERB.

King smiled at this. No doubt his reputation as a hard man and a strict disciplinarian gave pause to those who made their living in the grey spaces of Star Law. He was fair, to be sure. He always played by the rules. One could not succeed in his various lines of business and not do so, but he also knew how and when to change the rules to suit his own advantage.

As soon as the silvery sleek ship entered the docking bay, King forgot all about the middlemen of his latest purchase. He felt a sudden pang of pride and almost childlike reverence as he looked on an actual Ranger-class ship for the very first time in his life. Most had been scrapped, recycled, or scuttled in the wake of the Battle of Draconus Prime, later to be replaced by the larger, faster Paladin-class gunships. But those armored brutes just didn't have the sexy lines and grace of the earlier patrol craft.

"Sir," Jericho said, "my men are in position."

King frowned at the interruption of his moment. He looked up at the massive guard and sighed.

Jericho was the son of a human Undoc colonist and a Tel'klik soldier. Though he had his mother's smooth, furless skin and pale green eyes, he had inherited his father's hulking musculature and simian-like features. The orphaned half-breed had been raised by the Sisters of the Sun in a secluded monastery near Orion's Belt before escaping the cloister to join Star Cav.

Assigned to the same ship's crew, King had instantly admired Jericho's devotion to order, discipline, and particularly his religious zeal for punishing whatever he perceived to be wrongful activity. Naturally, when King had parted ways with Star Cav, he had brought his subordinate with him into his new vocation in private corrections.

"Very good. Let us greet our new guests." He led Jericho and Braun down the gangway to the bay floor where the *Ranger VII* was docked in a horizontal position, its thrusters and fins secured in gigantic magnetic locks. Four squads of heavily armored men wielding blast-proof riot shields and stun cannons surrounded the ship.

A hatch opened on the ship's underside and a muscular man in a form-fitting blue spacesuit dropped gracefully to the deck. Though he wore twin blasters on his gun belt, he made no move to draw. He was followed a moment later by the tall, lanky form of the blue-skinned Mechtechan.

Again, King gasped at these legends become reality. Though, in all honesty, he had expected the Last Star Warden to be taller.

"What's the meaning of all this? Who's in charge here? I've got a bone to pick with you." The Warden's voice boomed through the landing bay, filled with all the authority and presence King might have expected.

"I am Commandant Stanislaus King. This is my first officer, Ilsa Braun, and my head of security, Jericho. I welcome you to the Hulk 13, Star Warden." He stepped forward, Braun and Jericho at his back. King smiled, genuinely pleased to meet these two strangers. He found himself hoping that they would peacefully accede to his plans, and there would be absolutely no need for the unpleasantness of which he and his staff were more than capable. The unpleasantness for which they had already meticulously prepared.

However, if this man's reputation was based on fact, King knew there was small chance of that ever happening.

"Keep your welcome, King. You brought us here under false pretenses, so what do you want?" The Warden kept his hands loose at his side, close to his holstered weapons, but not close enough to provoke an attack. Though his head didn't move, King suspected the Warden's unseen eyes were assessing the tactical situation behind his visor.

Nor did the alien move save for the tiny antennae wiggling on his high forehead like hungry worms. King kept glancing at the tall creature, awed and unsettled by the unblinking black eyes, the expressionless mouth on the nose-less face. He was utterly fascinated by the last of the Mechtechan in this dimension.

"I have a business proposition, Warden. If you and your friend would care to join me for dinner, we can discuss the particulars."

The Star Warden raised his square jaw. "Just ate, thanks. Let's hear your spiel now, if you don't mind. That way we can be on our way as soon as possible."

King bristled. "Very well. I want your friend, here, to help me develop new technology based on that possessed by the Mechtechan. I have connections in various… fringe retail markets where such technology would command a very high price. We could all become ridiculously wealthy with very little effort."

The Warden glanced at the alien. When the Mechtechan slowly shook his head, the Warden said, "There you have it, King. We're not interested. But thanks for the 'invite.' Maybe just give us a call next time."

"I'm afraid I don't take no for an answer, Warden."

"And I was afraid you'd say that." The man's blasters cleared their holsters before the sentence was finished.

King blinked as Jericho grabbed him and hauled him behind a blast shield. He heard the sizzle of blaster bolts and stun rays and the cries of wounded men.

"Don't kill them!"

Regaining his composure as Braun held him behind the shield and provided cover with her own sidearm, King looked up to see Jericho lead a rush on the retreating Warden and alien. Before, the two were overwhelmed by the swarm of armored guards; now, almost a dozen wounded men lay stretched out on the deck.

"You should have had two detachments ready, sir," Braun offered.

He glared at her. "I should have pumped their damn ship full of gas as soon as they landed."

The Warden shook his head, trying to fight off the weakening, nauseating effects of the stun rays. He looked around, realized he was being carried between a pair of armored guards, his hands shackled behind his back. They followed a huge, hulking figure down a long, dark corridor. It was Jericho, the big guy who had led the charge that had clobbered Quantum and himself before they could reach the *Ranger VII*. The Warden thought he had hit the bruiser in center mass with at least one blaster shot, and yet there he was. Not even limping.

"Where's... my friend...? Where's... Quan... tum?" The Warden's speech was slurred, his face hurt. He had a feeling not all that pain was the result of a stun ray.

Jericho turned and sneered as they reached a heavy PermaSteel door. "You should worry about yourself, Warden. We're putting you in with Hogan for the night. Hogan don't like roommates, so you'll most likely be dead come morning."

The guards laughed as the door opened onto a pungent darkness. They tossed him in without ceremony, and without undoing his shackles.

When the door closed again, the Warden was all but blind. His visor had been removed from his cowl, so all he had to rely on were his senses of sound, touch, and smell. The last of these being punished by an overwhelming stench.

Someone moved in the darkness to his left. Someone big.

"Well. Look'ee here," a deep, guttural voice said. A small light flicked on. "Sorry 'bout the smell. I don't get facility privileges until next month."

The Warden blinked at the sudden glare, studying the big, middle-aged man in the ratty jumpsuit sitting on a filthy bunk—the only one in the cell. The man's hair and beard were long and braided, and had probably once been blond or light brown, but were now a dun color streaked with iron grey. A spider's web of deep lines surrounded dark eyes set in a leathery face.

But what drew the Warden's immediate attention was the tattoo on the man's big left deltoid. It depicted a single silver world silhouetted against a bright gold star, the planet's orbit balanced by six golden sunrays. It was the emblem of the Star Wardens.

"I take it you're Hogan," the Warden said with a grin. "Think you could give me a hand with these shackles?"

Hogan returned the grin with a mouth full of broken, discolored teeth.

King smiled as he entered the dark, sterile interrogation room. Jericho had just finished securing the Mechtechan to the PlaSteel Y-shaped upright gurney. Braun stood at the control panel, checking the power levels and bio-connections.

The bound alien watched the entire process with inscrutable detachment.

"As I understand it…" King rubbed his hands together and stepped to face the subject. This Mechtechan was the only one left in this universe, and he now belonged to Stanislaus King. "The Warden calls you 'Quantum.' A human affectation, I take it?"

"It is. My language vibrates on a soundwave barely tolerable to most lifeforms of this dimension."

King shook his head in fascination. "I did not know that, and I know more about the Mechtechan than anyone else in the galaxy."

"A false supposition." The blue alien seemed to study King rather than the other way around. "As I am clearly *in* this galaxy, it is an obvious deduction that I know more about my own kind than do you."

King chuckled and waved the observation aside. "I know, for example, about the spies your people first sent into this dimension. I know about the scouts who infiltrated and took over the agricultural colony on Tau Gamma Six, utilizing a mechanical means of mind control far more subtle and effective than anything the Tuatha ever developed.

"If it hadn't been for a pair of Star Wardens stopping in the colony for repairs and stumbling onto the plot, the Mechtechan invasion would have been well underway in the Frontier long before the U.P.C. could have mounted a suitable response."

The alien finished the story without emotion. "Instead, the Star Wardens were able to locate the breach from our dimension and strike while our Armada was in a bottleneck situation."

The unblinking black eyes turned to the control panel, then to the connections on its wrists and abdomen. "I assume you mean to torture me. Might I ask the reason?"

"Your technology. That mind-control device I just mentioned, for example. Do you know how useful that would be to humans? Why, I could ensure absolute obedience on this ship, planetary governments could secure their regimes in peaceful perpetuity, and corporations could vastly increase the productivity and compliance of their workforces.

"That invention alone would be as good as printing my own credits." King leaned close to the suspended Mechtechan. "Just help me build something like that, and there will be no torture. I promise. Then, once we're done, you and the Warden can go on about your business, or stay here as my partners. It is all up to you… Quantum."

"I was a science officer in the Mechtechan Armada. Not an engineer. It was my duty to collect, analyze, and process data, and to use that information to produce hypotheses and calculated projections. I am skilled in normal technical assembly and repair, but the design and production of the devices you seek are not within my skillset… Again, you have made a false supposition. I am no more capable of giving you what you want than you are of producing healthy offspring."

King stiffened. He'd learned from transcripts that some of the veterans of the Continuum War believed the Mechtechan possessed uncanny senses, able to see, hear, smell, and even taste on a much wider spectrum than most inhabitants of this dimension. Some of the veterans even believed their enemy had been psychic. Had this Mechtechan prisoner somehow sensed the deficiency in King's body, or was he merely referring to the fact that King was not a woman?

King turned to Braun and nodded. "Begin the data collection."

As his first officer activated the scans, King glared at the alien. "Well, this is not a 'false supposition,' my friend. I know that you have remarkable regenerative qualities that put most of our modern nanotech meds to shame. This means two things to me at the moment." He raised a finger to the impassive blue face. "One, your harvested bio matter will fetch a high price on several black markets."

King smiled, his voice high and shrill as he raised the second finger. "And two, I can take my time with you… Jericho, fetch my kit…"

"How do you live like this?" The Warden asked Hogan as the cell block's lighting came up. Hogan's contraband penlight had revealed only a fraction of the squalor and filth of the tiny room. "This is inhumane."

Hogan shrugged as he stood and stretched. "You get used to it… Still better than Tartarus."

The Warden raised an eyebrow. "Tartarus?"

"The lowest decks, the original prison wings. About a year after King took over operations, he shut them off from all contact, left them with nothing but bare minimal life support."

Hogan ran a gnarled hand through his filthy hair. "You ever read old Christian religious scripture, Warden? Jesus talks about a place of 'outer darkness with weeping and the gnashing of teeth' quite a few times. I reckon that's what Tartarus must be like, but nobody knows for sure…

"If you get tossed down there—for insubordination, fighting, too many demerits, or just because King or Jericho are having a bad day—you never come back."

Hogan turned to the door as a muffled loudspeaker announced breakfast. "Well, the screws'll be damn sure surprised to see you alive and well this morning. Worth not killing you in your sleep just to see the looks on their faces when they have to unshackle you."

Though the inmate had said this last with a playful wink, the Warden was not reassured.

During the night, Hogan had told him that he had once been a Star Warden in his youth, decades after the Battle of Draconus Prime. But, seeing the writing on the wall and knowing that the agency was soon to be replaced by the new Star Cav, he had opted to use his position and authority to feather his own nest before the end came.

But when that end arrived, and the growing corruption of the Star Wardens was exposed, scapegoats had been required. As luck would have it, Kal Hogan, Star Warden Second Class, had been tapped for the chopping block.

The onetime lawman had spent almost thirty years locked up in Hulk 13, about as many years as he had lived free. The Warden may have felt sympathy for Hogan, even gratitude for the man not taking advantage of his injuries and fetters during their initial meeting, but he knew he could not trust him.

"You losing your touch, Hogan, or just getting lonely?" One of the guards asked when the cell was opened. "Figured for sure you'd have painted this cesspit with the new guy's guts."

Hogan laughed as they undid the Warden's shackles. "I'm still thinking about it."

They were marched out to stand in a line with the other inmates, most of whom kept craning their necks to get a look at the newcomer in the relatively clean blue spacesuit. Unlike the correctional facilities of the Warden's time, there was no uniform attire for the prisoners. Each man looked as if he still wore the filthy remnants of whatever clothes he had had on his back the first day of his incarceration. Any attempt at hygiene appeared to be undertaken solely by the individual, and this only on a limited basis. It was clear to the Warden that whatever funds the U.P.C. allocated to Hulk 13 for the care of its inmates were being misappropriated.

As the line marched to the mess hall, the Warden wondered how much medicine and clean clothing could have been purchased for what King had paid the mercenaries to capture him and Quantum. The thought of his missing friend filled the Warden with guilt. If he had followed Quantum's suggestion to fight the disguised bounty hunters, they may have avoided this mess.

And now there was no telling what the corrupt and merciless King was doing to get what he wanted from the Warden's friend. He needed to discover where Quantum had been taken and find a way to free him.

The mess hall was an open area with rows of PlaSteel tables and connected stools spiraling out from a central guard tower. This was occupied by four men behind shatterproof GlasSteel windows. These presumably operated the surveillance cameras and automated stun cannons mounted in the upper corners of the big room. Two mezzanines encircled the mess hall, patrolled by a dozen armed men in riot gear.

The Warden noted that these guards did not carry stun weapons, but lethal blasters.

"If you're planning something," Hogan whispered as they got into the chow line. "This ain't the place to try it. All the common areas are designed to be meat grinders. There was a riot the first month after King took over. The Silver Knuckles; maybe you've heard of 'em? Cutthroat pirates. Anyway, they were the gang who used to run this place, and they decided to test the new commandant."

"What happened?"

Hogan held up his tray for a splash of greenish slop that looked like algae that had gone bad. "Well, let me put it to you this way. There ain't no living Silver Knuckles in this prison anymore. In fact, there ain't no gangs at all. King ain't big on inmate fraternization. If it looks like three guys are getting it in their heads to start up a club, the next thing you know, two of 'em are banished to Tartarus."

The Warden accepted this information with the same zeal as he accepted his helping of rancid proto-nutrition. The only thing that kept him from slipping into a dark mood was the sight of a tall, blue-skinned figure entering the mess hall from the opposite side of the room.

He motioned for Quantum to join him and Hogan, but when his friend sat down at the table without a tray, the Warden's rage threatened to boil over.

Quantum's eyes, usually a shiny black, were a charcoal grey. His pale blue skin was marred by several big purple bruises. And his left antenna was missing.

"What in the Sam Hill...?" the Warden said through gnashed teeth. "Are you okay?"

He thought Quantum smiled. "It is nothing, my friend. Commandant King and I have been discussing military history and theoretical mechanics. Nothing with which to concern yourself. As you know, I am quite resilient."

The Warden pushed his tray in front of Quantum. "At least eat something to keep up your strength. As I'm guessing you didn't give him what he wanted, I doubt he's through with you."

The nostrils on the top of Quantum's head puckered, his remaining antenna flicked back. "I believe this might do more harm than the Commandant's ministrations."

It took a moment for the Warden to realize his friend was joking.

King stood in his office, watching the live feeds from the cafeteria on his holo monitors. He was surprisingly grateful that the inmate Hogan had not killed the Warden as expected. It gave him an opportunity to see the Mechtechan subject converse in a more natural manner. He hoped it would give him some insight into the alien's mindset.

Of course, he was no fool and had little patience for playing patronizing games. He would get what he wanted from this Quantum, or both he and the Last Star Warden would be wiped from existence.

A chirp at the office door alerted King to Braun's arrival. "Come."

"Good morning, sir. The night shift has finished their scan of the Star Warden's ship."

King frowned, turned to see the smiling woman holding a data pad at her side. He really did wish he could find a young man with her devotion to duty and intelligent skill set. "Very good. What did they discover?"

Braun glanced at the pad's screen and flipped through the readout. "Aside from the vehicle being in excellent condition despite its age, it has been modified to a vast degree. The engines and weapons are now on par with modern technology, as are most of the sensor arrays and shielding. From what the chief engineer says, it appears these modifications are above even his level of skill."

King rubbed his chin. "So, our Mechtechan friend is actually a skilled engineer after all. I shall have to bring this matter up during our next chat."

"There is also a rather large data file on the ship's logs that our people can't decrypt."

King raised an eyebrow and almost smiled. "Really? Now that does pique my interest." He turned back to the visual display of the alien talking with the Warden in the cafeteria. "Have Jericho set up the interrogation room again. I think Mr. Quantum has had quite enough of a reprieve."

When a teeth-jarring buzzer signaled the end of breakfast, the inmates stood and hurried to bus their trays before lining up. As the Warden joined the queue, he saw Jericho, King's pet bruiser, enter the mess hall with four armored guards. They made straight for Quantum.

"Don't," Hogan whispered. "It ain't worth it."

The Warden didn't listen. He stepped between the approaching armed men and his friend. "Where are you taking him?"

Quantum touched his shoulder. "This is unnecessary. I shall go in peace."

"I'm not letting them cut on you again."

Jericho sneered and motioned to his men.

The four guards came at the Warden with stun batons, but he was ready. The first was unconscious before he hit the floor. The second became a shield, stunned into senselessness by the third man. When the Warden disarmed the fourth, using his weapon against him, the inmates began to get rowdy. Cheers turned into a chant of, "Warden! Warden! Warden!"

Pulse blasts shook the air as the stun cannons dropped over a dozen haggard men to the floor in spasming agony.

"That is quite enough, Warden." King's voice boomed from the loudspeakers. "Unless you want my men on the mezzanine to use lethal force to quell your little riot, I suggest you stand down."

The Warden dropped the stun baton and let go of the guard he used as a shield.

Jericho motioned for the recovering men to take Quantum into custody, then stepped forward and hit the Warden in the throat with his stun baton.

As the Warden convulsed on the floor, the stun baton continually reapplied to various parts of his body, he heard Jericho announce to the hall: "This man is not a hero. He is not your savior. He will not free you. He can only get you killed. Or worse. He can get you sentenced to Tartarus."

Following his men and Quantum out of the mess hall, Jericho finished the proclamation with, "I trust you all to do the right thing."

The Warden tried to stand, but nothing worked. As his consciousness began to fade, he saw a ring of filthy, haunted faces descend upon him.

"You have not been entirely truthful with me, Quantum."

King stood over the alien restrained to the horizontal Y-shaped gurney. Though still showing signs of trauma, the Mechtechan appeared in far better trim than the toughest of inmates who had faced similar treatment in the interrogation room. King suppressed a chill of delight at the thought of how long this process might last.

"I have spoken no falsehoods." The alien's dark grey eyes did not blink.

"And yet your silence has contained volumes of duplicity." King picked up one of the antique surgical scalpels he favored for such work. The electric shocks, while satisfying for a moment or two, left no visible testimony for later admiration. "You claim not to be an engineer, and yet the modified *Ranger VII* is a tribute to your technical prowess. Would you care to clarify?"

The Mechtechan continued to lock gazes with him, not flinching from the blade now hovering above its marred face. "Imagine a small child brings you a pencil drawing of a family standing outside a house. The people are amorphous collections of ellipses approximating limbs and torsos with curved lines and semicircles representing smiles and eyes, and the house is an irregular rectangle topped by an equally irregular triangle half the size of the largest person.

"Given this crude representation of a portrait, could you not make vast improvements on this picture even without the benefit of formal artistic training?"

King cracked a smile. The alien was easily the most intelligent being he had ever encountered, and yet here it was, trapped and under his power. Captured by King's own plans and ingenuity. "All right, we'll come back to that in a moment. Tell me about the encrypted file on the ship's log. What is it?"

The Mechtechan said nothing.

King slid the point of the scalpel against the edge of the big left eye. "I am serious, Quantum. It cost a lot of money to hire those bounty hunters. Not to mention the risk of the operation. If they had been intercepted by actual Star Cav ships before recovering you, I doubt they would have kept my name out of things. So, I'm going to ask you once more. If you do not answer, you lose this eye. Now, what is on that encrypted file?"

"What have you done with the Star Warden?"

King frowned. "I believe he is facing 'inmate justice' at the moment. If I am right, he is on his way to the lowest decks, and you will never see him again."

"Free him and I will tell you everything."

King stood straight, his hand quivering. He had to catch his breath, realizing he was torn between the desire for the alien's knowledge and the impulse to cause it more pain. Keeping his eyes on the prisoner, he stepped to the wall com and called Jericho. "Bring me the Warden."

"Sir?"

"I said, bring me the Last Star Warden. Now!"

"On my way. Jericho out." King could tell by the reluctance in the man's voice it was probably already too late.

The Warden came to his senses gripped by a dozen strong hands. He was carried aloft on a sea of unwashed bodies, descending into a darkened corridor. They held him so tightly he couldn't move his head. All he could see was the dimming light panels along the hallway's metal ceiling. Above the cursing and growling of the angry horde, he heard a familiar voice close to his left ear.

"I told you it wasn't worth it," Hogan hissed. "Now we've got to send you to Tartarus, or King will send some of us. I'm sorry, Warden, but you made your bed…"

Something was roughly shoved into his hand.

He heard a hatch open. He was fed into unwholesome darkness. The Warden tumbled down a ramp as the hatch slammed shut above him.

All light died.

He came to a painful stop on a slick metallic surface. The stench made Hogan's cell seem like a country garden after a warm spring rain. The Warden covered his face against the revolting miasma, praying that the ship's air filtration system still neutralized any airborne pathogens spawned in the unseen filth of this lower deck.

Touching the object in his left hand, the Warden realized it was Hogan's penlight. He flicked the device on and struggled to his feet. One sweep of the narrow beam revealed that the inmates' dread of this place was well and truly justified. Even the Warden's heart was chilled at this testament to humanity's ultimate degradation.

The walls of the chamber were splashed and caked with blood. There were sigils and graffiti written in the stuff, and the age-old motto: ABANDON ALL HOPE. Three pyramids of human and humanoid skulls stood as tall as the Warden's chest, and one corner was a reeking cesspit of rotting tissue. It did not take much imagination to understand on what sustenance the denizens of Tartarus survived.

A drum sounded in the distance, echoing weirdly through the darkened bulkheads. A long, ululating, and demoniac howl answered. The Warden shined the light around the grisly chamber until he found an opened door. He stepped through it just as he heard the first hurried footsteps. From the feral calls and growling sounds combined with the slapping of unshod feet on the deck becoming a quiet thunder, it seemed as though several dozen were racing to find him.

"Fresh meat," the Warden muttered as he broke into a run. Enveloped in the fetid darkness, he fled from the approaching and unseen horde.

The penlight flashed wildly around the narrow corridor, revealing scattered bones along the deck, walls stained with more filth and gore. The Warden could see there was no power run to any of the panels on this level, not even emergency lighting. But there was air, and he knew that King would not bother to keep a separate system running for the areas of his prison he deemed abandoned.

That meant one universal air system served all of Hulk 13.

That system was the Warden's only hope of escape. He had to find an access point, get inside, and pray that his instincts could guide him back to the upper levels and out of this nightmare. He just had to do it before the inmates of Tartarus found him.

He ran through the hellish labyrinth for what seemed an eternity. His pursuers never seemed to flag, their maniacal howls and insane gibbering echoing weirdly in the darkness, their hot breath fouling the already rancid air. The Warden's lungs and legs burned, his eyes ached from straining against the stygian gloom, but he could not stop to rest.

Resting meant death. And not a clean death, either. Not at all.

A grunt to his right warned the Warden of the strike a second before it would have skewered him. He swerved away as the blade of a makeshift spear lunged out of a hidden alcove. Flashing the penlight in his attacker's face, the Warden grabbed the weapon's shaft, wrenching it from its blinded owner.

The spear appeared to be made from the elongated chitinous forelimb of one of the sentient insectoids of the Elysium system. The Warden drove the blunt end of the weapon into the bewildered tatterdemalion's forehead, dropping the unfortunate soul to the deck.

The rabid pursuit grew closer. Shrieks of insane glee filled the corridor and his ears. The Warden waved the penlight in that direction. Scores of pale eyes glimmered in the distant shadows.

Taking the captured weapon, the Warden ran.

He hadn't gotten far before the penlight began to blink.

Every other heartbeat was in total darkness.

The gibbering howls and stampeding footsteps of his hunters boomed closer.

The stench of their hot and hungry breath and their filthy bodies choked the air.

The Warden came to a T-junction. On instinct, he turned to the right. The corridor narrowed, turned again, passed half a dozen sealed doors, and came to a dead end.

The light blinked faster, stayed dark longer.

The howling horde reached the first junction. Even if they split up, at least twenty or more insane criminals hungry for his blood would be upon him in moments. The Warden placed the penlight on the floor, ready to use the primitive spear and the narrow corridor to make his last stand.

He almost laughed at the notion of a man who had spent his life among rocket ships and ray guns perishing with a stone-age weapon in his hands.

The penlight's beam fell on an air grate in the floor.

The spear's blade made short work of the cover's seal. The Warden slipped into the ventilation shaft, doused penlight in hand, just as the maddened pack thundered over the closed grate. He held his breath and slid slowly away from the access point as his hunters went into a frustrated frenzy, turning on each other.

As blood dripped through the grate behind him, the Warden shook his head in pity. The inmates of Tartarus had been reduced to less than animals by King's callousness and cruelty. No one deserved that level of dehumanization and debasement, no matter their crimes. The Warden would make King pay for all he had done, but to do that, he first had to escape Tartarus himself.

He crawled through the darkness, searching for a way up. Up would lead him out. But once he was out, he would still be locked inside the worst prison ship in the galaxy. What he would do at that point was a bridge yet to be crossed.

"But cross it I shall, because Quantum needs my help. And Stanislaus King is long overdue for a reckoning."

"Three days." King paced the width of his office. "Three days, and still no sign of the man." He cast a furious glare at Braun and Jericho, both standing at attention just inside the door. "And yet we've lost how many down there?"

"Seven, sir." Jericho frowned, stared at the carpeted floor. His face was filthy, as was the riot armor he wore. He had led almost every shift of searchers down into the lower decks, only stopping to rest and eat at Braun's specific orders. "Seven dead. Thirteen wounded."

"Pathetic, Jericho! If Braun were a man, I'd send her down there. How do you like that? I'd prefer to send a girl than you at this point! You're useless!" King punched the palm of his left hand. "Double the shifts."

While Jericho continued the manhunt and Braun maintained operations, King had vented some of his frustration on the captured Mechtechan in the interrogation room. But the alien still refused to cooperate until it knew the Warden was free. "I want that man found, dead or alive."

Braun cleared her throat. "Sir, staff morale is very low. Dangerously so, I'm afraid." She went silent, but it was clear she wanted to say more.

King sneered. "Spit it out, woman. Speak your mind."

Braun took a deep breath, an action King found unseemly as it made her ample bosom seem to swell. "Well, sir, there are men on this ship that are due leave. Past due, in fact, and in light of the recent casualties, those men are… requesting that their leave be honored. I recommend we do so, at least for those with seniority. Set up a rotating schedule to assure the men that we still hold their best interests at heart."

King scoffed and resumed his pacing. "I should sanction desertion in a time of crisis? What kind of advice is that? About what I'd expect from a woman! Things get hard and you want to get all soft and comforting! Unacceptable! This is a prison, not a cruise liner!"

He looked at Jericho. "Take the names of the men 'requesting' leave, and make sure they are on the next search party. Tell them that if they ever want to leave this ship again, they must first bring me the Last Star Warden."

He glanced at Braun, now chewing on her pouty lower lip. "You want to improve morale, do you? Well, tell the men that the first crew to find our wayward Warden will receive two weeks paid leave and a thousand credit reward. That should motivate them to do their damned jobs!"

The Warden was so exhausted he almost didn't notice it.

The clean smell of fresh air.

Every bone and muscle in his body hurt, cramped and bruised from his interminable sojourn through the labyrinthine guts of the prison ship. The penlight had died some time ago. He didn't know exactly how long, just as he didn't know how long he had been crawling like a blind worm through the narrow metal tunnels. He judged it had been a matter of days by the growth of stubble on his face and the roiling hunger pangs in his empty belly. His mouth was bone dry, his throat filled with razor blades with each painful swallow.

But he had not stopped moving. Every ounce of his will focused on drawing and keeping a map of the ventilation system in his mind. It was not a perfect map. There had been a few mistakes, costly wrong turns and backtrackings. Costly in calories and time, neither of which could he afford to lose. But he did not stop, would not. Not even for a moment's rest.

Every time he thought he was done, out of energy, out of hope, he would close his eyes and see the battered and marred face of Quantum. He knew that no matter what his own troubles, his friend was being beaten and tortured by the madman who ran this flying hellhole.

Those few moments of hopelessness and despair would vanish, replaced by the Warden's resolution to rescue Quantum and to punish Stanislaus King.

When he tasted the fresh air on his face and tongue, the Warden opened his eyes and saw light for the first time in almost forever. He blinked against the pain that was brief yet euphoric. He wanted to laugh, but even the act of smiling split his dry lips and caused him to cough. He clutched the air grate with both hands to push through and into the outer corridor.

The muscles in his forearms and back knotted into fiery cramps and the air rushed from his lungs in a shuddering gasp.

"Who's there?"

The Warden held his breath.

It had been a woman's voice.

He thought he might have lost his mind somewhere in the winding dark and was imagining things. But then he heard a booted step on the deck outside the grate. Blinking to clear the crust from his eyes, he peered through the slats to see the blonde woman he had seen with King upon entering the Hulk 13.

Braun, he thought her name was.

She was alone.

The Warden realized he hadn't the strength to free himself from the duct. Not at present. He had a choice to make: wait for her to leave and hope his strength returned before Quantum died, or take a chance on this woman having some remaining sense of morality that might outweigh her loyalty to King.

He paused.

As he stared at her through the PlaSteel grate, just a meter away from possible freedom, the Warden's mind filled with memories of every wicked and evil thing, every act of duplicity and selfishness he had seen since his return to the Frontier. All these crimes paled in comparison with the horrors he had witnessed on this ship.

The woman turned to go.

"Wait…" The Warden's voice was barely a whisper in his own ears. He tapped the grate with his bloody knuckles. "Wait."

He blinked. The woman's lovely blue eyes stared at him through the narrow slats. He watched as her full lips slowly curved into a smile. "There you are."

The Warden returned the expression. "So I am."

"You have not found him."

King gritted his teeth at the smug expression on the alien's face. At least he imagined it was smug. The damned thing never showed any emotion at all, no matter how many wounds King inflicted upon it. The nub of a new antenna rose from the blue cranium just above the empty left eye socket. And still the Mechtechan gave him nothing.

"Do not judge yourself too harshly," the alien added, letting its head lean back against the gurney's padding. "He is an altogether unpredictable human being. Which is, to my mind at least, a considerable thing."

King removed his uniform tunic as he stepped into the interrogation room and began rolling up his shirtsleeves. "Is that a criticism of your friend?"

"An observation. Perhaps a critical one, but also one of admiration."

King opened the tigerwood case containing his antique surgical equipment. "Oh? You are actually capable of admiration?"

"Certainly. I am a scientist, after all. I am filled with wonder and awe every time I witness something new, unusual, or anomalous. I believe the more prosaic of you humans call them... miracles."

King scoffed. "You think your Star Warden is a miracle?" His hand hovered over the array of shiny steel scalpels, skinning knives, and amputation saws. He wondered whether something more severe was now in order.

"I said prosaic humans might think so. In fact, I have met several who do. What about you, Commandant? What do you think of the Last Star Warden?"

King turned back to face the alien. He frowned. "Me? I think he is a madman with delusions of grandeur. I think he is an egomaniac feeding on his ever-growing legend. I think he would be nothing without your help and your technology, Quantum. I think he stirs up trouble where there is none and then makes a name for himself when he 'saves the day.' Just like the riot he started in the mess hall, leaving the inmates to clean up his mess and you to suffer for his stubbornness.

"In a word, I think him a nuisance."

The alien smiled. An actual smile. "He certainly can be. I have seen him stand and fight when the logical option is to flee, and I have seen him surrender when fighting would provide the better chance for success. When he makes these irrational decisions, his only defense is simply to say, 'It is the right thing to do.' What I find so maddening is the fact that, more times than not, he is usually correct.

"Yes, my friend can be a nuisance at times. But he is, in my estimation, a significant variable in the cosmic equation. A particularly important and positive variable that balances out a great many negative integers."

King picked up a pair of chrome-plated snips. "For example?"

"Why, you, of course." The one-eyed, blue-skinned alien smiled wider. "When all is said and done, the Warden will remove you from the cosmic equation, Commandant. So do your worst while you can, you will not get my secrets. And if you do not seek atonement, you will most certainly pay for the crimes you have committed.

"My friend will see to that."

King's face rippled with rage as he raised the snips to the alien's three-fingered left hand. The rage grew stronger when he saw the Mechtechan watching him with that same passive, detached expression.

The Warden opened his eyes and groaned.

He sat on a chair covered with a bedsheet. His wrists were encased in gravity shackles in his lap. Directly across from him sat the blonde first officer, "Braun" stamped in red on the left side of her black riot vest. She held a blaster pistol leveled at him.

He glanced around the room and saw they were in a rather spartan berth.

Clearing his throat, he said, "I hate to disappoint you, Ms. Braun, but I'm not in the habit of entering a young lady's quarters on the first date."

She smirked. "Plucky for someone who looks like he just crawled out of hell on his belly. Pluckier still for someone with a pistol aimed at his heart."

The Warden smiled. "That first bit is a pretty accurate description of the past few days. As for the second part..." he shrugged. "Well, let's call it an occupational habit."

She shook her head. "You're the real deal, aren't you? The honest-to-Cosmos Last Star Warden. 'The Specter of Sinister Space.'"

The Warden stretched his neck, tested his muscles. The cramps were greatly diminished, and he didn't feel quite as dehydrated, but he was still famished. A glance at his filthy spacesuit explained the bedsheet. "Well, to be honest, you're not catching me on one of my better days. I usually cut a much more dashing figure... So, why am

I here and not back in Hogan's cell or locked up in solitary or something?"

Braun's delicate brow furrowed and she chewed her lower lip. "Because, Warden, you have brought me to a crossroads in my career." She absently flicked the weapon. "Or rather you find me at one to which I'd already come."

The Warden nodded. "I'm listening."

Braun placed the blaster on the small table between them and stood. She paced around the tiny room as she spoke. "My parents were ex-Star Cav. After they got out, they scraped together some money and bought an old Housecarl-class freighter. Dad pulled some strings to get a contract hauling supplies to Cav forts along the Frontier. Somewhere along the way, they decided to add kids to the mix. Me first, then a year later, my brother Helge.

"By the time I was old enough to enter Star Cav Academy—my dad's biggest dream was that his kids would be officers and not grunts like him—we had three ships, and my folks were about ready to retire to the Civilized Worlds and run the business end of things. Helge would enroll in the academy the following year. But before that, they had one last haul before handing things over to a hired crew.

"I was in my first month at the academy when I got the news." Braun stopped and stared down at the Warden. "The Silver Knuckles hit them just as they exited the ERB in the Sigma Prime system. It was three days before Star Cav realized the shipment was late and sent out a search party... Three whole days. The Knuckles had taken their time with them. There were no open caskets at the funeral..."

The Warden watched the hatred and pain pour out of the woman, could feel it. "The Silver Knuckles. They used to run this prison from the inside, right?"

Braun's blue eyes flicked as if suddenly remembering he was in the room. "Yes.

And as soon as I heard what King did to those bastards, what Star Cav had failed to do, I left the academy and came here. I've been devoted to him ever since."

The Warden kept his eyes on her, knowing the pistol within easy reach was a test. "But now you're having second thoughts. You've seen King for what he is, a madman and a sadist."

"He's a monster." Braun narrowed her eyes. "I've always known he didn't really respect me, but he did appreciate me. And that used to be enough...

"I even accepted his corruption and graft, somehow convincing myself he deserved the money for what he'd done to the Silver Knuckles, what he continued to do to the worst criminals in the galaxy... And so long as I believed that the men on this ship, the prisoners, *were* the worst in the galaxy..."

Braun shook her head. "But after seeing what he's willing to do to the guards who have been so loyal to him, after seeing what he did to your alien friend—"

The Warden sat up. "Quantum? What has he done to him? Is he still alive?"

Braun frowned. "Yes. He has something King wants, and King is far too thorough and patient to kill him before he gets it. That's the tragedy of it. Your friend Quantum's regenerative abilities make him the perfect plaything for King's insatiable cruelty. I can't imagine..."

The Warden tried to stand, felt his head go light and fuzzy. Colors zipped across his vision. "I've got to get him out of there. I've got to stop this..."

Braun put a hand on his shoulder to steady him in the chair. "You're not going anywhere until you've had about three more rounds of hydro meds."

"You don't understand. King wants access to Mechtechan technology. If he gets it, he could tear a hole in reality. Trust me, you don't ever want to see that."

Braun raised her chin. "Fine. As soon as you can stand up without falling over, you can go save the universe and your friend. But you're not going alone."

"We've cleared out all of Tartarus," Jericho said. The armored brute smelled of filth and burnt petrol. They'd used flamethrowers to complete the sweep of the lower decks. "There's nothing alive down there. No sign of the Star Warden. Can I dismiss the two teams you've got guarding the interrogation room?"

King sat at his desk, hands stained with purple blood folded on the glass-topped mahogany wood. He shook his head, wondering how this endeavor had gone so terribly wrong. He had paid the bounty hunters a small fortune—a wise investment given the prize to be gained. He had purchased the bogus Star Cav ident codes from a reliable, if pricy, black-market dealer, and had even authorized the expansion of his security staff in the weeks leading up to the capture.

"And he still won't talk." King glanced at the small stainless steel bowl containing three blue fingers and sighed. "No matter what I do to him, he still won't give me an inch. I can't deprive him of sleep, he seems to need little if any food, and he is all but impervious to pain.

"I've never encountered anything that I can't break to my will…"

"Sir? The teams?"

King looked up at Jericho, realizing he was still there. "No sign at all? Not a fresh corpse, a shred of blue spacesuit, a square-jawed skull? Nothing?"

Jericho shook his massive head. "No, sir. He's just vanished."

King slammed his fist on the desk. "Impossible! I've heard what they call him, but the man is not a ghost! He is still on this ship somewhere, and you need to find him. The sooner, the better. Do you understand?"

"Yes, sir." Jericho bowed and turned to leave.

"Put another team on the interrogation room. And tell Braun I want to see her!"

Alone in the office, King's eyes drifted to the huge flickering painting of *The Battle of Draconus Prime*. "If I can't force this Mechtechan to give up its secrets, I'll have to buy them. But the only thing it wants is the Warden's freedom… Or is it?"

Snapping his fingers, King grabbed his tunic and headed for the interrogation room. The stick had failed miserably, so it was finally time to try the carrot.

The right one this time.

After the hydros, a nutrient bar, and a hot shower, the Warden felt somewhat human again. He hadn't wanted to waste time on the ministrations, but Ilsa Braun had insisted. And since he had no chance of success without her help, the Warden had reluctantly complied. She had even retrieved a new spacesuit, visor, and his gun belt from the *Ranger VII* while he showered.

"All right," he said buckling on the twin Comet blaster pistols. "Let's go get Quantum."

Ilsa still wore her riot gear and sidearm. She gave him an approving smile. "You're right, you do cut quite a dashing figure on your better days."

The door chirped, slid open. Jericho entered without waiting for an invitation.

For a moment, the three of them stared at each other.

The Warden reached for his right Comet, but Ilsa was in the line of fire.

Jericho drew his own blaster.

"No!" Ilsa grabbed the guard's hand and tried to disarm him. Jericho lifted her off the deck easily, tossing her into the wall with enough force to dislodge the framed pictures.

In the same moment, the Warden launched himself across the tiny berth. His right hand locked around Jericho's throat. His left grabbed the gun-wielding wrist. His right knee drove into the guard's armored groin.

The onslaught knocked Jericho off balance and into the opened doorframe but had little other effect. The big guard grinned before his left fist came down on the Warden's right trapezius. The blow knocked the Warden's right hand loose, his entire arm going numb.

Hooking his right heel behind Jericho's, the Warden threw his weight into the man's midsection. Jericho, already off balance, tripped and went down, the Warden still gripping the blaster-wielding wrist for all he was worth.

The two grappled on the deck, exchanging short, ineffectual blows. Each moment Jericho's greater strength slowly brought the blaster pistol closer and closer to the Warden's face. Looking up, the Warden realized Jericho's head was across the sliding door's threshold.

Spinning his torso across the big guard's breastplate, the Warden kicked the door control panel. The PlaSteel door slid from its wall sheath and slammed Jericho's skull into the doorjamb with a sickening crack.

His eyes rolling back into his head, the big man went limp. The blaster fell to the floor.

"Is he dead?" Ilsa stood above the Warden as he struggled to regain his breath.

The Warden hauled Jericho into the room and checked his pulse. "No. But he'll have a heck of a headache when he comes to."

Taking the gravity shackles from Jericho's belt, he locked the unconscious guard's hands behind his back. Then, fetching Ilsa's set, he used them to bind Jericho's feet. "I don't know how long he'll be out. Can't have him sounding an alarm before we're done."

Ilsa stared at the unconscious Jericho, strange emotions in her eyes. "I know you must think him no more than King's thuggish henchman. I suppose to a certain extent, he is." She looked at the Warden. "But he's also a kind and innocent soul. I think King took advantage of that innocence and made him into the brute you now see."

The Warden dusted off his suit and checked his pistols. "Yet another crime for which Stanislaus King must pay."

Ilsa nodded. "Yes. Since Jericho is here, maybe King is alone in his office. Come on."

The Warden followed the first officer through the narrow corridors of the prison ship. Surprisingly, they encountered no staff or guards.

Ilsa commented on this. "I'm guessing those not on duty are hunkered down in their quarters. If they're not afraid of you, they certainly are of what King might force them to do in order to find you."

"Quite the inspiring leader. Though I suppose it is easier to cultivate morale and loyalty when everything is in your favor."

King's office was locked, but Ilsa knew the passcode, and they moved quickly inside the luxurious room. The Warden was stunned at the opulence nestled in the heart of such a hellish place. Thick carpet and marble flooring, walls paneled in exotic wood, antique furniture, and a bookshelf filled with rare leather-bound tomes. Trappings that would have been considered "retro" even in his own time. But he was almost overcome by the faithful three-dimensional rendering of the greatest conflict of his life.

"He's not here." Ilsa stepped to the desk. "Oh, my Cosmos…"

The Warden turned from the painting to see what had drained the color from her face. His jaw and fists clenched when his gaze fell on three severed blue fingers in the stainless steel bowl. With shaking hands, he unbuckled his gun belt.

"What are you doing?" Ilsa looked at him.

Carefully placing the twin Comet blasters on the leather seat of the high-backed chair, the Warden took a deep breath. "If I'm wearing those when I see King, I might just kill him. And that would not be justice."

Ilsa frowned as she pulled up a report on King's desk. "You might reconsider that. He's tripled the guard on the interrogation room. There's thirty of Jericho's best men in riot gear, armed with blaster carbines between us and your friend. I'm betting the Commandant is there as well."

"Any chance you can get them to stand down?"

She pulled up another program on the desk. "No. Based on the command log, they've been instructed to answer directly to King alone. But I can help with the odds, somewhat."

She brought up another menu and typed in a few commands. "One thing about prison-issue blasters, they all have a kill-code linked to their serial numbers, in case a weapon is captured by an inmate. I can access the kill program and neutralize those blasters, but the men will still have their stun batons."

The Warden dragged his gaze away from his friend's severed fingers. "Even without blasters, the two of us are no match for thirty armored men... But I have an idea."

"Ah, Commandant King. I thought we'd seen quite enough of each other today."

King forced a smile as he entered the interrogation room. "I fear, Quantum, that you and I have gotten off on the wrong foot. And I am fully prepared to admit that this is entirely my fault."

The alien tilted its head magnanimously. "That is... very big of you. And also a completely correct assessment of our current situation."

King pulled a hover chair over to the upright gurney. He kept the smile in place as he admired his handiwork. The Mechtechan was now a pale shade of turquoise, missing its left eye, all the fingers from its left hand, its right antenna (the replacement left was still regenerating), and its right ear. Its naked body was covered with purple scars and bruises in various shades of violet.

And yet Quantum's undersized mouth returned his smile.

"I have a proposition for you," King said. He reached into the wall-mounted med kit and withdrew a hypo filled with a universal health booster. "Give me what I want, and I'll give you what you want."

The Mechtechan watched as King injected it with the dose designed to accelerate the natural healing process. "I have already declined your offer of financial gain, and you have failed to locate the Star Warden in order to grant his freedom... Unless that situation has changed?"

King shook his head and tossed the empty hypo into the recycle bin. "No, I'm afraid it is most likely that the legendary Last Star Warden is now just that, a legend and no more."

"I believe that assessment is the latest of your many false suppositions, Commandant."

King fought the snarl he felt curling his lips. "What I'm talking about, Quantum, is giving you what you really want. What you desire more than anything else." He leaned forward and stared hard into the one remaining grey eye. "You want to go home."

The alien's silence was King's first real success since he'd strapped the thing down in this room.

"Yes," King continued. "I know that's all you want. To go back to your own world, to be among your own kind, to be a part of your own society. It must be a living hell for you here. You are surrounded by what you can't help but consider a galaxy of mental degenerates, constantly bombarded with sensory input that doesn't suit your physiology, exposed to customs that must seem barbaric and silly. No matter what planet, moon, or station you set foot on, you will always be 'the alien.' You will always be imprisoned, after a fashion.

"It must get tiresome, if not downright depressing. Tell me I'm wrong, Quantum."

The alien swallowed. "You are not wrong, Commandant King. Not entirely…"

"Then help me build the machines I want, and we can work together to find a way to get you back through that black hole and back to your own kind."

When the Mechtechan leaned its head against the padded gurney and its rarely seen eyelids shut for several moments, King knew he had finally won. He had broken the alien, and he would get what he wanted. Just as he always did.

After the horrors of Tartarus, Hogan's cell wasn't quite as offensive as the Warden had first thought it to be.

Still, the rancid smell caused Ilsa to take a step back when she opened the door. "Are you sure about this? I think it's a bad idea."

"Of course it's a bad idea. It's a terrible idea. But it's the only one I've got." The Warden turned and called into the darkened cell. "Rise and shine. I've got a job for you, Hogan."

The disheveled former lawman shambled into the hallway, covering his squinting eyes with one hand. "Warden? Is that you?"

"It is. I owe you one for giving me that light. I might not have made it out of Tartarus without it. But right now, I'm afraid I need another favor."

The inmate smiled, revealing his ruined teeth. He blinked repeatedly until his eyes adjusted to the hall's illumination. "It does get pretty dark on this ship. They've had us on lockdown since we tossed you down there. No light…" Hogan licked his dry lips. "What can I do for you, Warden?"

"I'd like you to help me start a riot."

Hogan's jaw dropped. He looked to Ilsa for confirmation. "What?"

"You could call it a *coup d'état*. We're overthrowing King. Jericho is already out of the picture, but we've still got thirty guards to overcome."

When Hogan grimaced, Ilsa tapped her wrist chrono. "Don't worry about the blasters. I'll take care of those. It'll just be man-to-man."

The Warden clarified. "Armored men armed with stun batons. That's why I need you to pick the strongest and most reliable of the bunch. We can't afford to let everyone out. As soon as King is in custody and we have control of this ship, we are turning everything over to Star Cav.

"You will all still be prisoners, but I can promise you that I'll do everything in my power to see that you get the humane treatment you deserve. Perhaps even get the U.P.C. to convene a committee on prison reform."

Ilsa added, "And I will testify on behalf of those wrongfully incarcerated at King's direction. Hopefully, I can undo some of the wrongs I've been a party to."

Hogan grinned, puffing up his chest. "Well, it's been a while since I busted some heads. Can't promise I'll be any good in this fight, but I'll damn sure give it a go."

The Warden smiled. "Good. Now, who can we trust?"

Hogan laughed. "Not a soul, Warden. Not a soul. But I know a few guys who'll count it a blessing to get a fair crack at the screws, even if it means dying."

The Warden shook his head. "I guess that'll have to do. Come on."

It took King a moment to realize the Mechtechan had lost consciousness. Another moment to realize it wasn't breathing. The next moment panic set in.

"Cosmos!" King jumped from the hover chair and looked from the alien to the med-kit, unsure of what to do. "The booster! I should have checked the medical chart. The nanites are programmed to accelerate cell repair in creatures from *this* dimension!"

He flipped the upright gurney into the horizontal position, then raced to the control panel. His fingers fluttering across the virtual keyboard, King hurried to pull up the medical data as quickly as possible. "No, no, no, no, no…"

He was so close to finally getting what he wanted. Technology that would not only allow him to be the master of this galaxy, but also give him inroads to others. And he may have just killed that glorious future with the absent-minded application of a hypo. King growled through clenched teeth. "Why did I do that? Just goes to show that mercy is never a good idea…"

The Mechtechan's medical scans filled the holo screen. King skimmed the information. "Damn. Got to get him to sickbay." He tapped the command that undid the gurney's automated tethers. He was halfway to the supine alien when he heard shouts and the sounds of battle outside the interrogation room.

He looked up at the monitor displaying the outer corridor to see the Last Star Warden leading a mad rush of over a dozen ragged inmates in an assault on his armored guards. For a moment, he couldn't understand why his men weren't using their blasters. Then he saw that his first officer, Ilsa Braun, was with the rioters.

"The inconstancy of women…" King drew his sidearm. The one issued to him by Star Cav many years ago, and thus not subject to penal-facility kill codes.

The Warden entered the long corridor leading to the interrogation room alone. "I heard you guys were looking for me."

The armored men at the other end of the hall jumped to attention, raised their blaster rifles. Their helmed heads swiveled, looking to one another for the next move. They had been ordered to protect the alien, but they had also been ordered not to kill the Star Warden if he turned up.

The Warden walked straight at them, his steps getting quicker the closer he got.

He was almost on top of them before one of the men shouldered his weapon with the intent to fire. When the carbine hummed and gave a dry click, the guards knew they were in trouble.

The Warden hit the mass of men like a thunderbolt. He knew they were just doing their jobs and were not responsible for the travesty of justice he had seen on this ship. At least not entirely. Still, he had a lot of aggression built up, and the sentries stood between him and the man who was responsible.

More importantly, they stood between him and his friend.

At least four guards were incapacitated before those in the rear ranks drew their stun batons. The Warden retrieved one of the devices from a downed sentry, turned it on the next man in the pack, and prayed Hogan and Ilsa weren't dawdling. He tried not to think too hard on the fact that he, a career lawman, had just pinned his hopes for success on freeing over a dozen convicted felons.

A baton connected with his ribs and the Warden recoiled. Pain and nausea swept through his body, muscle spasms threatening to topple him to the floor. Deflecting the next strike with the haft of his weapon, the Warden spun the attacker into the path of another baton's strike. Still another weapon came over this falling opponent, grazing the Warden's left shoulder.

A gloved hand caught him as he staggered back in agony.

Gasping for air, the Warden smelled the horde of filthy inmates just before they hit the broken line of sentries with a high-pitched, banshee-like scream. Hogan was in the lead, a recovered stun baton in each gnarled fist.

The Warden turned to see Ilsa smiling as she pulled him out of the thick of the fray.

"You've done your part, Warden. Let these men blow off some steam." She gave him a wink. "Besides, if too many of them are still on their feet at the end of this, we might have another kind of problem on our hands. Hogan could start a riot for real with his experience and charisma."

The Warden frowned as he caught his breath. "I take your meaning, but I got these men into this fight. I'm not leaving them to it." Pushing off from the wall, he launched himself back into the battle.

King stood facing the door. He had locked it, but Braun could override the passcode. His lip curling, he only hoped she would be the first one through the door. He would put a bolt in her belly. "And while she bleeds out, I'll put two in the Star Warden's smug, handsome face."

"Do you really think he is handsome?"

King turned to see the naked blue Mechtechan towering over him. There appeared to be no evidence of the torture which King had inflicted upon it in the past several days. No missing parts, no scars, not even a single bruise or blemish.

"I suppose there is a certain symmetry to his features which most humans find appealing. However, I must confess, you all look terribly similar to me."

"I—I thought you were dead…" King heard himself gasp the idiotic words as he raised the pistol.

Quantum knocked it from his grasp with the ease of disarming a child. "As I wanted you to think, Commandant. I determined that I had gathered sufficient data from this experiment, and it was time to end it."

King backed away from the freed alien. "But… but I know I hurt you. I cut away parts of you."

The Mechtechan moved gracefully, shadowing him. "Mere biological matter. Even without benefit of the booster hypo, which I recommended you give me, I would have fully recovered in due course. As I hope you are now well aware, Commandant King, my race is far superior to yours in every conceivable way."

"Y-you recommended?" King struggled to understand. "You influenced my mind!"

"Subliminal communication." The rangy Mechtechan stalked him around the room like a hunting feline. "It is typically only useful for observing members of other species, determining their individual personalities and subconscious proclivities. However, I have long suspected that its use might be made more proactive through the in-depth study of an individual. Hence, this experiment."

The alien's pitch black eyes blinked, and the tiny mouth smiled. "I have been studying you very closely over the past few days, Commandant, and your mind, your very identity, is an open book to me."

King moved the gurney between himself and the Mechtechan. Struggling to swallow down his growing fear, he tried to reason with the thing. "But we can work together, Quantum! We can send you home!"

The alien tossed the gurney aside and grabbed King by the front of his tunic, lifting him until his jackboots left the floor. "Ah, yes. Another of your false suppositions, Commandant. I told you that you were not wrong in your argument for my isolation and misery, at least not entirely."

Quantum drew King close, eye-to-eye. "Yes, I do wish to return to my own world and be among my own kind. And yes, the vast majority of this universe's inhabitants are significantly less advanced than myself, and many—such as yourself—can be 'barbaric and silly.' But I do not find it a 'living hell' as you put it, and as you now see, my physiology is more than adequate to deal with any stimulus your dimension can provide.

"But the primary reason I do not find this universe 'tiresome' or 'downright depressing' is that even if I am always 'the alien' on every planet, moon, or station in this universe, I have a friend who does not consider me so. To the Star Warden, I am a brother."

King's mouth worked but no words came to mind. How could this *thing* be considered a friend, much less a brother by any human being?

"That's right, and brothers take care of one another."

King turned his head to see the Star Warden standing in the interrogation room's opened door, Braun and a handful of tattered and bloodied inmates behind him. All wore satisfied, smug looks on their detestable faces.

The Warden turned a warm smile to the Mechtechan. "Sorry it took so long. Are you okay?"

Quantum's fully-restored antennae wiggled, the big black eyes shining. "I am very well, my friend. Just ending a rather educational experiment here."

"Please," King said to anyone who might listen. "Don't let it kill me."

"Kill you, Commandant?" The alien dropped him to the floor. "I am sorry you would ever think such a thing of me. No, sir. I believe it high time justice finally came to Hulk 13, which means you must stand trial for your crimes."

A week later, the *Ranger VII* left Fort Dawn, the Star Cav space station above Priam Four, and made for the nearest Einstein-Rosen bridge. Hulk 13, along with the flotilla of warships that had responded to Ilsa's S.O.S., remained docked on the installation. A military tribunal had convened to take testimonies and gather evidence for the pending U.P.C. investigation into the misdeeds aboard the prison ship.

The implicated staff were being held in custody to await trial.

"Well, I think Stanislaus King is going to find himself on the other side of the penal system for the rest of his life." The Warden sighed, grateful to be done with the experiences associated with his time on Hulk 13. "And I believe Kal Hogan will have his sentence commuted to time served. But one thing is for sure, that prison ship will be retired, and the inmates moved to more humane facilities."

"Are you concerned about the fate of Officer Braun?" Quantum asked. He and the Warden sat in the command chairs of the ship's small bridge. "She is facing rather severe penalties if she is not acquitted of the charges against her."

The Warden shrugged. "I gave them my testimony, telling them how she helped me recover after my time in Tartarus, and how she was instrumental in overthrowing King."

Quantum made a scoffing sound. "I suppose that would be true, had I not already been in control of the situation."

The Warden glanced at his friend with a raised eyebrow. "And how was I supposed to know that? Next time you embark on a psychological research experiment, let me know, will you?"

"Of course. Although in this particular case, it was a spur of the moment decision."

"I didn't think you were fond of those."

Quantum's mouth curved into a smile. "You must be rubbing off on me."

The Warden laughed. "Well, where to now? Draconus Prime, perhaps?"

Quantum looked out the forward view screen and was silent for a moment. "No."

His antennae twirled. "Not just yet. I believe there are many more pirates and outlaws in the Frontier that require our immediate attention."

The Warden typed in a set of coordinates on the nav computer. "Ever heard of a gang called the Silver Knuckles? I hear they like to work the Sigma Prime system."

"Then what are we waiting for?"

The *Ranger VII*'s thrusters released white atomic fire, and the silvery sleek ship darted across the infinite void, en route to the next adventure.

"I may just kill the next space pirate on sight."

The Last Star Warden looked up in surprise. Though Quantum had been a soldier in the Mechtechan interdimensional invasion force, the Warden had never heard his friend express such a bellicose sentiment out loud. "Something bothering you?"

Quantum slid into the *Ranger VII*'s copilot seat, his short antennae drooping. His oversized, shiny black eyes were narrowed, his undersized mouth flat. "Ever since we came through that wormhole ten months ago—as you reckon time—it has been nothing but one drama after another. Alien overlords, haunted space stations, outlaw gangs, rogue military units, illegal corporate experiments, and... space pirates. Where does it all end?"

The Warden smiled. "I think you're right. We need to take a break." He pulled up a display on the ship's console. "As luck would have it, we are just in time for the big Earth Day Festival on Nu Terra V."

Quantum raised one dubious antenna. "A human celebration?"

The Warden set course. "You'll love it. Nu Terra V was settled by refugees from the Sol system's last internal war some seven hundred years ago... Eight hundred, I have to remind myself... Anyway, the first colonists were survivors from all the various warring factions, so when they established their new world, they started a tradition to commemorate the best of their old one.

"Earth Day became a time to celebrate the brotherhood of humanity, a time to embrace one another as friends and family, and a time to put away all the foolish, selfish things that divided human beings. The celebration eventually grew until the

Earth Day Festival on Nu Terra V was legendary throughout the galaxy."

Quantum leaned forward, intrigued. "And what kind of festivities might this celebration entail?"

The Warden leaned back and crossed his hands behind his head, fondly recalling the Earth Day he had attended—over a century before by the calendar, but a mere decade ago according to his memory. "Well, there's the food, for starters. Folks make tons of their best recipes to share with everyone, and I mean everyone. Then there's the music: some of the most beautiful songs sung on every street corner by whole choruses of complete strangers. There's pageants and plays, parades and ballroom galas. Families give each other gifts, travel to visit distant kith and kin, gather to enjoy fine meals, play games and tell stories, and generally have a grand old time."

Quantum's glum expression gradually melted. "Sounds... interesting."

The Warden's smile widened as they passed through the Einstein-Rosen bridge that would take them out of the Frontier and into the fringe of the Civilized Worlds. "You'll love it."

"Are you certain this is Nu Terra V?"

The Warden checked the coordinates in response to Quantum's question. And in response to the strange planet they observed through the ship's GlasSteel canopy.

A blockade of huge ships surrounded a highly-industrialized world covered in massive stretches of urban development. The corporate freighters glimmered with enormous holographic billboards along their metallic hulls. These vigorous animations advertised all manner of goods, from tasty treats to top-end luxury ships. At a glance, the advertising campaign appeared to be the first line of battle among three uber corporations: Deeznu, Kronos-Wagner, and Argonaut.

The Warden frowned. "The coordinates are right. But this doesn't look like the friendly, low-tech world I visited my first year out of the academy."

Quantum's antennae twirled. "That was over a hundred of your solar years ago. As we've learned since entering this era, quite a lot has changed."

"Apparently." The Warden didn't add that he hadn't found much to be for the better. "Let's go see what's what."

A mosquito-like corporate interceptor flew out to head them off. "Approaching ship, please identify yourself and state your business on Nu Terra V."

"This is the *Ranger VII*. We are here to take part in the Earth Day Festival."

The corporate pilot's voice came over the coms after a short pause. "Please specify. Are you here for the shopping and entertainment, or are you here to visit the Shrine?"

The Warden raised an eyebrow. "*The* Shrine? Isn't Nu Terra covered in Earth Shrines?"

The interceptor pilot laughed. "Where have you been, *Ranger VII*? Most of the shrines were bought out over the past fifty years. The only one left is in the Deeznu Corporate Zone. If you want to go there, you'll need to dock with a Deeznu freighter and buy a visitor's pass. That'll entitle you to land in the DCZ and give you access to all Deeznu eateries, activity centers, and retail outlets. Transmitting the coordinates now... Happy shopping!"

Quantum gave the Warden what he interpreted to be a dirty look. "Your Earth Day Festival seems to be nothing more than an excuse to indulge in excessive commerce."

The Warden pulled on his suit's skullcap and eye-concealing visor. "So it would seem."

After purchasing the Deeznu visitor's pass (at quite a hefty sum), they landed at the specified corporate zone's starport. Quantum suggested they turn around and go back to the Frontier, even if it meant running across more space pirates. But the Warden had a burr under his saddle and wouldn't let the degeneration of the Earth Day Festival go without first getting some answers.

Disembarking, they set out to find the last Earth Shrine on Nu Terra V. The DCZ was a terrestrial version of the corporate blockade orbiting the planet. Every building was alive with animatronic or holographic advertising, and every street was lined with markets, vendors, stores, bodegas, restaurants, eateries, VR parlors, gift shops, and every other commercial venue one might imagine.

Where the Warden remembered carols and hymns, he now heard sales pitches and jingles. The scent of flash-fried, mass-produced fast food replaced the aromas of homemade, fresh-baked goods. The décor which had once celebrated the origins of a unified people was now dedicated solely to which venue touted the best sales. Worst of all were the people themselves.

Instead of smiling faces greeting them with hails of, "Happy Earth Day!" or, "Be blessed, brother!" the Warden and Quantum were bombarded with shouts of, "Out of the way! Can't you see I'm in a hurry!" or, "Look out! Big boxes coming through!" Though all the folks seemed quite affluent, judging by the copious amounts of shopping bags and boxes each of them carried, not a soul looked remotely happy.

Quantum sighed. "Are you sure you would not rather go find some space pirates?"

The Warden scowled. "Come on. I see the shrine up ahead."

The towering Earth Shrine was an elegant white pagoda with sweeping lines and graceful arches surrounded by tall pines, firs, and spruces. As they drew near, the Warden saw that the place was in poor repair and the evergreens needed tending. It was also the only place along the busy street devoid of patrons. Outside the gate stood a faded sign: EARTH DAY PAGEANT! COME AND EXPERIENCE THE JOY AND PEACE OF A TRADITIONAL EARTH DAY CELEBRATION! (CONTRIBUTIONS WELCOMED)

The courtyard was occupied by a handful of individuals singing as they built a temporary stage, sewed theatrical curtains, and painted large canvas backdrops. These happy workers were supervised by a tall, dark-skinned woman with elegant coils of graying black hair trailing down the back of her long white vestments.

She turned to face them with a warm smile. "Hello, and welcome to the Earth Shrine. I am the Guardian, but you can call me Octavia. What joy can our humble shrine offer you, strangers?"

The Warden returned the woman's smile, relieved to finally see some shadow of the holiday cheer he had hoped to find on this world. "Hello, Miss Octavia. I'm the Star Warden, this is my friend Quantum. It's been a long time since I've been to Nu Terra V, and I was hoping you could tell me exactly what happened to Earth Day."

Octavia tilted her head. "*The* Star Warden? The man out of time and space? Shouldn't you be on the Frontier, engaging in some mythic act of derring-do?"

"We're on holiday," Quantum said.

With a chuckle, the Guardian invited them to walk with her in the Shrine's well-tended garden. She told how the festival on Nu Terra V had become so famous that people from all over the galaxy would come to celebrate, bringing their money with them. As the shrines and the population grew ever wealthier from these annual events, it wasn't long before the world's leaders decided to extend the festival, first by an extra week, and within a decade by another month, until finally, Nu Terra V "celebrated" Earth Day year-round.

"This was just the beginning," Octavia continued as they reached the high-ceilinged sanctuary at the Shrine's heart. Beautiful, animated 3D images of Earth and the Sol system hung in the air of the polished ivory room. "It didn't take long for the corporations to see how much money could be made by throwing their hats into the Earth Day ring. And the world leaders, already wealthier than our ancestors could have ever dreamed, saw the opportunity offered by corporate partnerships. They let the wolves in the door."

The Warden folded his arms. "In less than a century those partnerships turned into buyouts... turned into that out there."

Octavia looked at the slow-spinning holographic Earth and smiled sadly. "Yes. And now we are the last independent shrine on this planet... But not for long."

The Warden raised his chin. "How's that?"

"The land upon which the Shrine sits is owned by the original colonial charter, held in trust. That trust recently dissolved when the local government transitioned into the Deeznu Corporate Zone. We have three days to raise seven million credits to purchase the land, or the Deeznu Corporation will annex it. Then this shrine will go the way of all the others, just another money-making attraction."

"Three days. Earth Day. That's why you're putting on the pageant."

Octavia nodded. "It's our last hope. So far, we've raised almost sixty thousand credits, but we are running out of time."

The Warden exchanged glances with Quantum. The alien gave a resigned shrug. "What can we do to help?"

A volunteer stepped into the well chamber. "Octavia? A lady from the press is here to see you."

The Guardian smiled. "As it happens, your arrival is quite timely. We need the media to help spread the word far and wide about our pageant. Perhaps you could share your memories of what Earth Day once meant with our visiting journalist?"

"Be happy to. And Quantum and I know our way around hand tools, so we can pitch in with the chores."

"Thank you both so much." Octavia led them to the courtyard where a blonde woman in a stylish green jumpsuit stood in the glow of a hovering cam-bot's lights, speaking with a pair of volunteers. "After I've talked with her, I'll send her your way."

The Warden nodded at Quantum. "Well, let's get to work."

"Absolutely. I often crave manual labor while on vacation. I find it far more relaxing than enjoying a good meal or taking in the local entertainment and scenery..."

Sometime later, as the Warden and Quantum raised a platform on the finished stage, the reporter came by. In a whiskey voice more suited to the blues than broadcasting, she said, "Hello. I'm Danica Stone, with the Intergalactic News Service. Might I ask you some questions?"

"Certainly." The Warden hopped down from the stage, smiling at the attractive woman. Her eyes were the same shade of emerald as her jumpsuit and her crooked smile was just this side of perfect, making her seem more like the girl next door than an unapproachable media goddess. "We'd be happy to talk to you."

Miss Stone motioned the cam-bot into position where its bulbs painted them in brighter hues. Turning a smile to the artificial eye, she said, "I've got a surprise guest here at the Earth Shrine on Nu Terra V. Rumored to be the Last Star Warden, this mysterious man has volunteered to help with the preparations for a *traditional* Earth Day celebration."

The way she stressed "traditional" gave the Warden pause, as if she were about to tell a joke. One he wouldn't like. "Yes, that's correct. I brought my friend Quantum to show him an Earth Day Festival like the last time I was here. But… quite a lot has changed since then."

Miss Stone continued to smile at an unspoken joke. "So, that would have been when, exactly? Is it true what the rumors coming out of the Frontier say about you? That you were lost in time for over a century?"

The Warden nodded. "That about sums it up. Yes."

She turned back to the camera with the equivalent of a wink. "So, you admit to being behind the times, then. What, in your opinion, could an old-school Earth Day pageant possibly offer to a modern audience? What can the Shrine present to people used to 4D holographic projection screens and VHD surround sound home theaters? How can untrained volunteers possibly put on a better show than professionally-rendered CGI characters voiced and performed by award-winning artists?"

The Warden cleared his throat. But the young lady and her audience were spared his intended lecture by a disturbance at the front gate. Five big men in dark clothing forced their way into the courtyard. They wore respirators over the lower parts of their faces and carried heavy sledges in their hands.

"Everybody out!" one of the men shouted. "Get out!"

The volunteers that hadn't been flattened in the initial invasion scattered. Octavia moved to confront the men. "What do you want? We don't keep money here, and our artifacts aren't worth much by modern standards."

The Warden and Quantum hurried to join her, though both had replaced their gun belts with tool belts. "You guys are in the wrong place," the Warden said. "That is, unless you came to help us build sets for the pageant. In that case, glad to have you."

The leader extended his hammer at the Warden's face. "Ain't going to be no pageant, stranger. So you and your blue pal best shove off before we make an example of you. Stay out of our way and nobody needs to get hurt."

The Warden glanced at Octavia. "Guardian, you might want to get your people to cover. This is about to get ugly."

And it did.

The Warden and Quantum waded into the sledge-wielding thugs like a pair of rock crushers in an asteroid field. Unarmed as they were, the two veterans of the Continuum War proved more than a match for ruffians used to intimidating folks by sheer size and swagger alone. In a matter of minutes, the five men tucked tail and ran or limped from the shrine.

"Shall we pursue them?" Quantum asked, wiping blood from his knuckles.

"No. Doesn't take a genius to figure they were hired by Deeznu. Probably freelance muscle paid in cash so as to leave no paper trail, no legal strings. Nobody else has a motive to prevent the pageant."

The Warden rubbed a growing bruise on his jaw as he surveyed the damage. The men had made use of their superior numbers to keep the Warden and Quantum occupied while still managing to destroy a significant portion of the sets and decorations. "Looks like we won the fight but lost the war."

Octavia and the volunteers walked through the wreckage, hollow and broken expressions on their faces. "There's no time," the Guardian said quietly. "There's no time to start over. And our coffers are bare…"

Danica Stone and her hovering cam-bot stepped close to the Warden. "What will you do now?"

He scowled, not having a good answer. "Something. I don't know what just yet, but something. We're not quitting."

At least he had the satisfaction of seeing Danica Stone without a jaded smirk on her face.

"I cannot believe every store in this zone refuses our commerce," Quantum said. "Almost as much as I cannot believe your offer to replace the damaged sets out of our dwindling funds."

The Warden shrugged. After the row, they had helped Octavia and the volunteers make the most of the aftermath. Danica had departed to edit her footage.

"I'm not surprised. Deeznu has an effective monopoly here. Word is out that we're trying to help the shrine, which is in direct opposition to the corporation's agenda. So we'll have to go further afield to buy new materials. I'll take the *Ranger* back up to the freighters and buy a commerce pass to another corporate zone. In the meantime, see what you can do here."

"Very well. Just try to stay out of trouble."

At the starport, the Warden was unpleasantly surprised to find someone waiting for him on the *Ranger VII*'s launch pad. "Can I help you, Miss Stone? I thought you'd have gotten enough footage at the shrine to finish your hit piece on 'old-school' traditions."

"I suppose I deserve that. But I'd like to know more. More about you, certainly, but also more about what's going on here. I'll admit the only reason I came to Nu Terra V was to interview you, and I couldn't care less about the shrine or the festival. But now—"

"How did you know I'd be here?" The Warden paused before climbing the gangplank.

The reporter gave a small smile. "Let me go with you and I'll tell you what I know. Then you can fill in the gaps. Maybe together we can see the bigger picture."

The Warden frowned, gave a curt nod. "Come on. But this'll be a short flight. Even shorter if I think you're trying to play me."

"Fair enough."

As they strapped in and the Warden began the pre-flight system checks, Danica said, "I heard you say something about those thugs working for Deeznu. What if I said you were wrong about that?"

The Warden raised an eyebrow behind his visor. "Okay. You've got my attention."

"I believe they may have been hired by Argonaut. The same company that, technically, I work for. INS is a subsidiary of Argos Entertainment, which is a branch of the uber-corporation. Somebody at Argos sent me the tip about your ship entering the corporate blockade. By the time I entered the system, they had fed me the info about you looking into the Earth Shrine situation."

Firing up the *Ranger VII*'s rocket thrusters for liftoff, the Warden said. "Why would Argonaut want the pageant to fail if Deeznu will reap the benefits?"

Danica visibly struggled against the G-forces as the ship rose from the launch pad and climbed into the planet's atmosphere. "Because… they want me to paint Deeznu as the big bad in a David versus Goliath story… If Deeznu is tied up in a PR fiasco during the height of the shopping season… it could mean a windfall for Argonaut's final fiscal quarter of the year."

The Warden chewed on this, but not for long.

Blaster bolts arced past the ship.

"Looks like whoever sent those thugs to the shrine just upped their game and their budget." Blue sky faded into eternal night as he pushed the ship higher into the upper atmosphere. The *Ranger VII* was designed for space flight and combat, whereas the attacker was a sub-orbital gunship, built for air support and dogfights in terrestrial warfare. "Strange to find one of those on a planet dedicated to commerce and entertainment."

Danica's face faded to white. "You really have no clue just how cutthroat the corporate wars are, do you?"

"Nope." The Warden pulled the yoke hard, knifing across the climbing attacker's path. The enemy craft fired again, but the *Ranger VII* spiraled and accelerated, moving between the fiery bolts without taking so much as a scratch.

When the gunship maneuvered to reacquire a pursuit angle, it turned onto its back, seemed to freeze in midair, and fell in a widening spiral. The sudden shift in G-forces coupled with the change in atmospheric pressures stalled the sky-ship's engines.

The Warden pushed the *Ranger VII* into a nosedive, chasing the falling craft back into the lower atmosphere at supersonic speeds.

Danica spoke through clenched teeth. "What are you doing? You're going to get us killed!"

The Warden focused on the target. "Got to get close enough to fire grapple lines so we can stop that fall. If that ship hits anywhere populated, it might as well be a bomb."

The plummeting ship's pilot didn't help matters. Panicked or discombobulated, his attempts to regain control only caused the craft to behave more erratically.

A voice came over the ship's coms: "Ranger VII, *this is DCZ air traffic control.*

Break off your approach or we will fire on you."

"Sorry, DCZ control. If I do that, a lot of folks down there are about to have a very bad day." Ignoring the sweat crowding the corners of his eyes, the Warden continued to accelerate until the targeting computer locked onto the falling ship.

Flicking the fire-control and hitting the trigger, he sent four harpoons trailing DuraSteel grapple lines into the target's hull. One of these carried a small EMP charge, shutting down the gunship's engines and controls.

"Got him!"

In a wide, marsh-edged clearing several kilometers from the DCZ, the Warden and Danica pulled the pilot from the rescued ship. Though he wasn't happy about the minor damage to his craft, the man was grateful his intended targets had saved his life.

In response to Danica's questions, the mercenary admitted, "I was hired through back channels to harass you on takeoff. Just a show of force to scare you away from the planet. I sure wasn't expecting to engage in a dogfight."

The Warden nodded. "You were paid in cash. I assume by Argonaut."

The pilot scoffed. "Doubtful. Those guys hate my guts. I used to work for them when I did legit jobs. They blackballed me. If I had to guess, I'd say it was Deeznu or Kronos-Wagner. Nobody else can afford me." He turned at the approach of wailing sirens. "But I guess we'll have plenty of time to discuss this on the way to lockup."

The Warden looked at the approaching patrol skimmers. "Miss Stone, would you be so kind as to relay a message to my friend Quantum? Can you tell him I managed to find that trouble he warned me to stay out of?"

Danica frowned. "But you're supposed to be a lawman. They can't take you in for this. We were attacked!"

The Warden smiled. "I've no jurisdiction here in the Civilized Worlds, and I wouldn't go so far as to call the system they've got here law, exactly." He watched as the flashing lights came closer. "You know, I used to love this place, even though I'd only ever been here once before. But that one visit, that one Earth Day Festival has stuck with me ever since…

"The camaraderie and good cheer, the *happiness*… It all reminded me what it means to be a member of the human race, to be a part of something so big, so different, and so important. It reminded me how no matter how bad things can get, how bad *we* can get, there's still a goodness in our nature… a love for one another that's always just beneath the surface, waiting to extend a helping hand, offer a kind word, or a supportive shoulder. Sometimes all we need is that reminder, and the Earth Day Festival was that for me."

He looked at Danica, noticing the hovering cam-bot for the first time. "But then, I'm just an old-fashioned kind of guy."

When the corporate enforcement officers arrived, the Warden raised his hands in surrender.

"Hope you've got a nice little nest egg put aside, Warden." The gunship pilot sat across from him in the prisoner transport. Both wore gravity shackles on their wrists. "They'll probably sentence us to some pretty hefty fines in the morning. Maybe even impound our ships. If you can't pay, then it'll be indentured servitude for the rest of your life."

"Nice." The Warden sighed. What he wouldn't give to be facing down a flotilla of space pirates at that moment. But then, he realized with a chuckle, in a way he was. But these pirates had not only plundered goods and property, they had pillaged the entire system of law and governance. How did the notions of right and wrong work when the very structures intended to safeguard society had been so corrupted?

He could only hope that Danica would have a change of heart and use her media resources and influence to do something about the pageant. If Octavia and the Earth Shrine won this fight against Deeznu, it all might actually be worth it.

The Warden's only regret was that Quantum could be stranded in this den of greed without a ship and without a friend who understood him. Even if the Warden spent the rest of his days slaving away in a factory or digging in a mine, he would be surrounded by others of his own kind. Quantum, forever separated from his own dimension, would always be alone...

After the hours-long processing (made even longer by his complete absence from any database known to the modern world), the Warden, aka John Doe 42, was finally ushered into a small holding cell on the thirty-fourth floor of the detention center. His small window looked out over Commerce Square, the heart of the downtown corporate zone. The wink and flash of neon advertisements colored the tiny room with multitudinous hues in a hypnotic rhythm. The roaring sound of countless overlapping ditties, skimmer horns, shouts, and general street cacophony eventually turned into a mind-numbing susurrus.

Stretching out on the hard bunk, the Warden stared at the ceiling tiles until he dozed off.

He was awakened by the sound of his own voice: "...offer a kind word, or a supportive shoulder. Sometimes all we need is that reminder, and the Earth Day Festival was that for me."

His words came from outside his cell window.

Standing on his bunk, the Warden was surprised to see his own visored face staring back at him from the big holographic billboard dominating Commerce Square. Danica had uploaded his speech, and the network was broadcasting it across the major channels.

The Warden watched as scores of early shoppers stopped and stared at his projected image, listened to his recorded words. When the speech was replaced by an ad for a new sports drink, the crowds returned to their business. A half hour later, his speech played again. This time the crowds were bigger, and the pause was longer. The cycle repeated twice more before a guard came to his cell.

"Sorry, fella. But your hearing's been postponed." The uniformed man placed a prefabricated meal on the small table beside the bunk. "Something about the bigwigs getting their heads together."

The Warden ate the tasteless breakfast and listened to the advertisements punctuated by his brief oration. By lunchtime, he noticed that less noise came from the square. Taking another look from the window, he saw that the crowds had thinned out to the point that actually using the word "crowd" could be considered an exaggeration.

By dinner, Commerce Square was a ghost town. The hypnotic sales pitches played to an empty house.

The Warden felt somehow optimistic as he settled in for the night.

He was awakened hours later by something he thought he'd never hear again. In fact, at first he thought he was dreaming, remembering. It was a carol. An old Earth Day carol extoling the virtues of brotherly-love, charity, unity, and compassion. The carol was sung by the loveliest soprano voice he'd ever heard. It was coming from outside, in Commerce Square.

The Warden got up, stood on his bunk and looked through the window. Guardian Octavia's face, twenty-feet tall, stared back at him from the titanic billboard across the way. She sang the carol. But she was not the only one. Far below, on the streets and sidewalks, a multitude of others joined in.

The sun was rising on Earth Day.

The Warden saw his own visored face on some of the smaller display screens in shop windows along the thoroughfare. His speech was still being aired.

Another voice with a now familiar whiskey-blues quality joined the carol. It came from somewhere outside the cell. The Warden turned as the door opened to find the security officer standing beside Quantum and the singing Danica Stone. All were smiling, even the guard.

"I don't understand," the Warden said.

"Your fine has been paid." The guard held out the Warden's gun belt and blasters. "And your ship is no longer impounded."

Quantum raised a data pad displaying the official paperwork. "You have Miss Stone to thank."

Danica laughed and shook her head. "I wouldn't say that. Let's just say the folks of Nu Terra V are as generous and good-natured as they've always been. They simply needed someone to remind them of that fact. And that someone was you, Warden."

The Warden smiled as he buckled on his guns. "You ran a story championing the Earth Shrine's pageant."

Quantum's antennae whirred. "She did more than that. The story suggested that people across the galaxy abstain from any commerce whatsoever to show their support for the Earth Shrine and the 'true meaning of the Earth Day Festival.'

"In less than twelve hours following the story's release, stock prices began to plummet across the board. By hitting them where it hurts, Miss Stone shamed the corporations into realizing what they had done to the festival, and by extension, the planet."

"Argonaut paid for your and the *Ranger VII*'s release." Danica took the Warden by the arm and led him from the cell. "And Kronos-Wagner put up the seven million to donate the land to the Earth Shrine. With that kind of PR *coup de grâce* stacked against them, Deeznu had no choice but to foot the bill for the pageant and its marketing. As I understand it, folks from all over the galaxy will be coming for the next week to experience a good, *old-fashioned* Earth Day Festival."

Stepping out of the detention center and onto the street crowded with hundreds of singing people, the Warden was astounded by the stark contrast with the day of his arrival. The crisp morning air smelled of sweet baked goods and warm cider. A total stranger smiled and slapped him on the back as he passed, shouting, "Be blessed, brother!" Another grasped his hand in both of hers and wished him, "Happy Earth Day! And thank you so much!"

Quantum leaned close. "So, are all human celebrations like this?"

The Warden laughed. "For the most part. Though the frequency of fisticuffs and incarceration varies from household to household."

Author's Note:
The Origin of The Last Star Warden

By the summer of 2019, I was utterly exhausted by the Pop-culture War, having seen most of my beloved franchises torched into burnt-out husks by Post-Modernism, Nihilism, and Identity Politics. Disney had turned *Star Wars* into the cinematic equivalent of fast food, CBS had taken the intelligent optimism of *Star Trek* and twisted it into a mean-spirited and poorly written parody, and the BBC had essentially told generations of *Doctor Who* fans, "We're taking this away and giving it to someone else because you don't think like we want you to."

I had given up on comics and superheroes years before, but they were faring no better. Though Alan Moore's *Watchmen* and Frank Miller's *The Dark Knight Returns* had been catalysts in making me the storyteller I am today, they had also turned the paradigm of the four-color superhero on its head. Attempting to emulate (or flat-out copy) these seminal works, an ensuing generation of writers and artists embarked on the systematic and industry-wide deconstruction of the hero.

And I had grown bone-tired of it all.

So, as I sat in a local auto dealership waiting on a factory recall, I brainstormed and doodled in my notebook. I set out to recapture what I had always loved about heroic storytelling and genre fiction. Naturally, I had to go back to the beginning—my earliest childhood heroes. Who were they and what about them had fascinated me at such an early age, and why were they essentially timeless? Why, so many decades later, did I still love them?

The Lone Ranger. My dad has always been a big western buff and, like most of my tastes in fiction, I inherited that from him. As a child of the 1970s, my favorite toys were the Lone Ranger and Tonto action figures from Gabriel. I watched the old reruns of the Clayton Moore TV show and was ecstatic when the Saturday-morning cartoon finally came along. I was even more so when I found out about the live-action movie in 1981, which I saw at the local drive-in theater when I was eight years old. I remember begging for the film novelization, and then having my dad go through and mark out all the "bad words" so I could read it.

But what was it about the Lone Ranger that so captivated me? Was it the blue suit and the twin six-guns, the mask? Probably. But I think it was also the fact that he was the Good Guy, so much so that he wouldn't even kill the Bad Guys. No matter how much harder it made his life, the Lone Ranger always did the right thing.

The Bat-Man. Like a lot of folks my age, one of the earliest memories I have of Batman comes from the Saturday-morning *Super Friends* cartoon. Another, of course, is from reruns of the old Adam West TV show. These incarnations share almost nothing in common with the grim and gritty Dark Knight of modern times. When I was a kid, Batman was the hero with the best gadgets and the coolest vehicles, but he also smiled and made jokes. And though there was plenty of *Bang! Pow! Zap!* action, as often as not, the Caped Crusader used his wits to beat the Bad Guys before sharing a laugh with Robin and Commissioner Gordon.

Captain America. I've always loved medieval knights even more than Old West cowboys. With his shield and chain mail shirt, Captain America seemed like the Marvel Universe's version of a modern-day knight in shining armor. As I got older and began reading his comics, I found that the comparison extended to his ethos as well. Cap, like the Lone Ranger, is the quintessential Good Guy. He's also a soldier, like my father and my grandfather, so I appreciated the military aspect of his character—the rigorous training and discipline, the drive to exceed one's personal limits.

And though Buck Rogers had done it decades before, Captain America is also a man out of time. He's a Greatest Generation character living first among the Baby Boomers, and now adjusting to Gen-Xers and Millennials. Yet, in his mind, and in mine, the Right Thing doesn't have an expiration date.

The Phantom: One of—if not the very first—costumed crime-fighters. Another two-gun hero in a mask on a white horse. A man with a mysterious origin and a legacy of immortality. A legendary man who fights pirates and corrupt governments. But a living, breathing man all the same. The fact that the character's mystique is built on family and lineage makes the Phantom a believable human being. We know that the man in the mask will die someday, but the Phantom and what he stands for, what he fights for, what he believes in, will live on. And the Bad Guys secretly tremble in that knowledge.

So, where to take this amalgamation of Wild West lawman, urban crime-fighter, super soldier, and jungle legend? Why, SPAAAAAACE of course! (Yes, Space Ghost was another obvious influence.)

Flash Gordon and Buck Rogers are Sam Jones and Gil Gerard in my mind, not Larry "Buster" Crabbe and, well, Larry "Buster" Crabbe… though I have watched some of the serials. But the proto/subgenre of the ray gun and rocket ship has its fingerprints on everything from *Forbidden Planet* through *Star Trek* and *Star Wars* all the way to *Farscape*, *Firefly*, and *The Expanse*. We, as human beings, love the notion of exploration, of reaching out to see what's "beyond." Infinite space will always be that: The carrot forever out of our reach. And that is why space adventures will always appeal to us in one form or another.

The Last Star Warden is a Good Guy. He is a lawman dedicated to doing the Right Thing, even if the modern worlds around him don't necessarily know what that is. He's a mortal man, alone in this quest save for his friend and one-time enemy, Quantum. The Lone Ranger had Tonto, Batman had Robin, Captain America had Bucky (and later The Falcon), and the Phantom had Guran. The Last Star Warden has Quantum, an interdimensional alien with a mind like a supercomputer.

Together, they battle the Bad Guys, wherever they find them. They're soldiers forever fighting The Good Fight.

In SPAAAACE!

About the Author

Jason J. McCuiston was born in the wilds of southeast Tennessee, where he was raised on a carnivorous diet of old monster movies, westerns, comic books, horror magazines, sci-fi and fantasy novels, and, of course, Dungeons & Dragons. He attended the finest state school that would have him with the intention of becoming a comic-book artist. This did not pan out, so following his matriculation and a brief and unprofitable stint as an illustrator of tabletop RPGs, he embarked upon a whirlwind tour of spectacularly underpaid and uninspired careers. Half a lifetime later, he came to his senses, realizing he was meant to be a professional storyteller.

Publishing his first story about zombies, kung fu, and family ties in Parsec Ink's 2017 *Triangulation: Appetites* anthology, Jason has been a semi-finalist in the Writers of the Future contest and has studied under the tutelage of bestselling author Philip Athans. His stories of fantasy, horror, and science fiction have appeared in numerous anthologies, periodicals, websites, and podcasts.

Project Notebook, his first novel, can be found with most of his other publications on his Amazon page at https://www.amazon.com/-/e/ B07RN8HT98.

Jason lives in South Carolina, USA with his college-professor wife and their two four-legged children, Grendel* and Winky. Connect with him on the internet at: https://www.facebook.com/ShadowCrusade. And he occasionally tweets about his dogs, his stories, his likes, and his gripes @JasonJMcCuiston.

*Editor's note: Grendel has since passed, but his spirit lives on in the Warden's faithful companion, Quantum. R.I.P. to one of the goodest boys ever.

A CELEBRATION OF STORYTELLING

The Anthological Festival of Tales

58 stories by 39 authors designed to honor the art of writing by
including a fair, festival, or celebration in each telling.
From fantasy to sci-fi, from thrillers to mysteries,
we know readers will truly enjoy this feast of fables.

Now Available from   Dark Owl Publishing, LLC

www.darkowlpublishing.com

SOMETHING WICKED THIS WAY RIDES

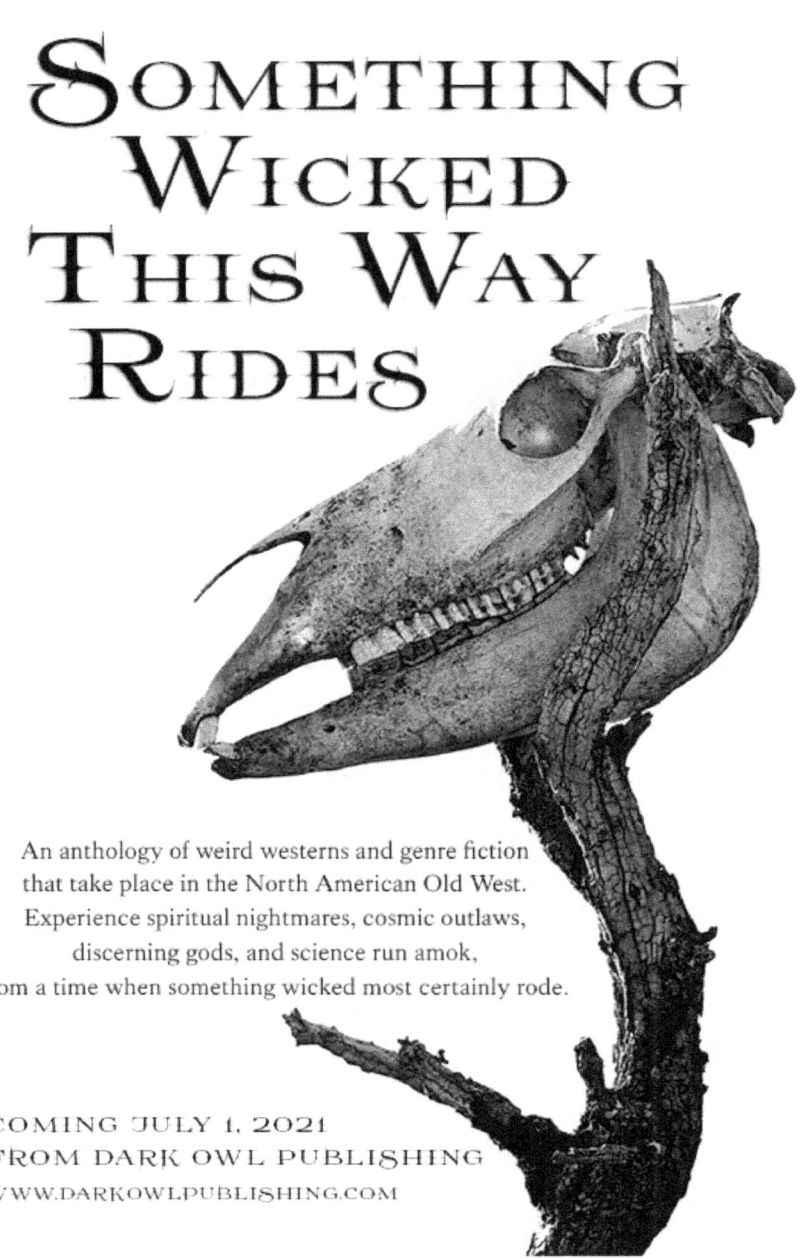

An anthology of weird westerns and genre fiction
that take place in the North American Old West.
Experience spiritual nightmares, cosmic outlaws,
discerning gods, and science run amok,
from a time when something wicked most certainly rode.

COMING JULY 1, 2021
FROM DARK OWL PUBLISHING
WWW.DARKOWLPUBLISHING.COM

THE DARK

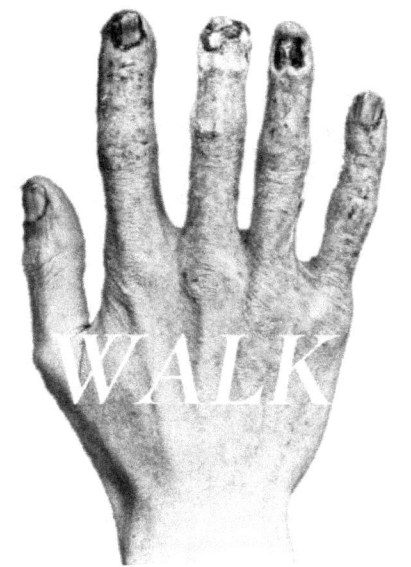

WALK

FORWARD

A HARROWING COLLECTION BY
JOHN S. MCFARLAND

Available in paperback and on Kindle from
DARK OWL PUBLISHING, LLC
www.darkowlpublishing.com

No Lesser Angels,
No Greater Devils

*Beautiful and haunting stories from
the unique and relatable prose of*

Laura J. Campbell

Coming May 1, 2021 in paperback and on Kindle

Dark Owl   Publishing, LLC
www.darkowlpublishing.com